THE HUNTING LION
OF CATHNE!

A lion was stalking Tarzan, a lion wearing the harness of a trained hunter. As it came nearer, it seemed vaguely disturbed. Its tail twitched; its head was flattened; slowly it came on, its wicked eyes gleaming.

Tarzan waited. In his right hand was a sturdy spear, in his left the hunting knife of the father he had never known. He measured the distance as the lion started its swift, level charge; then, when it was coming at full speed, his hand flew back and he launched the heavy weapon.

Deep beneath the left shoulder it drove, deep into the savage heart; it checked the beast's charge for but an instant. Infuriated now, the carnivore rose upon its hind legs above the ape-man, its great, taloned paws reaching to drag him to its slavering jowls.

The *Authorized Editions* of
Edgar Rice Burroughs'
TARZAN NOVELS
available in Ballantine Books Editions
at your local bookstore:

COMPLETE AND UNABRIDGED!

TARZAN
AND THE
CITY OF GOLD

Edgar Rice Burroughs

BALLANTINE BOOKS • NEW YORK

Tarzan and the City of Gold was first published serially in *Argosy* magazine, March 12 to April 16, 1932.

Copyright © 1932 Edgar Rice Burroughs, Inc.

ISBN 0-345-28987-0

This authorized edition published by arrangement
with Edgar Rice Burroughs, Inc.

Manufactured in the United States of America

First U.S. Edition: March 1964
Seventh Printing: April 1981

First Canadian Printing: May 1964

Cover painting by Neal Adams

CONTENTS

CONTENTS

1

Savage Quarry

D OWN out of Tigre and Amhara upon Gojam and Shoa
and Kaffa come the rains from June to September,
carrying silt and prosperity from Abyssinia to the
eastern Sudan and to Egypt, bringing muddy trails and
swollen rivers and death and prosperity to Abyssinia.

Of these gifts of the rains, only the muddy trails and the
swollen rivers and death interested a little band of *shiftas*
that held out in the remote fastnesses of the mountains of
Kaffa. Hard men were these mounted bandits, cruel criminals
without even a vestige of culture such as occasionally leavens
the activities of rogues, lessening their ruthlessness. Kaficho
and Galla they were, the offscourings of their tribes, out-
laws, men with prices upon their heads.

It was not raining now; and the rainy season was drawing
to a close, for it was the middle of September; but there was
still much water in the rivers, and the ground was soft after
a recent rain.

The *shiftas* rode, seeking loot from wayfarer, caravan, or
village; and as they rode, the unshod hoofs of their horses
left a plain spoor that one night read upon the run; not that
that that caused the *shiftas* any concern, because no one was
looking for them. All that anyone in the district wished of
the *shiftas* was to keep out of their way.

A short distance ahead of them, in the direction toward
which they were riding, a hunting beast stalked its prey. The
wind was blowing from it toward the approaching horsemen; and for this reason their scent spoor was not borne

7

to its sensitive nostrils, nor did the soft ground give forth any sound beneath the feet of their walking mounts that the keen ears of the hunter might detect during the period of concentration and mild excitement attendant upon the stalk.

Though the stalker did not resemble a beast of prey, such as the term connotes to the mind of man, he was one nevertheless; for in his natural haunts he filled his belly by the chase and by the chase alone; neither did he resemble the mental picture that one might hold of a typical British lord, yet he was that too—he was Tarzan of the Apes.

All beasts of prey find hunting poor during a rain, and Tarzan was no exception to the rule. It had rained for two days, and as a result Tarzan was hungry. A small buck was drinking in a stream fringed by bushes and tall reeds, and Tarzan was worming his way upon his belly through short grass to reach a position from which he might either charge or loose an arrow or cast a spear. He was not aware that a group of horsemen had reined in upon a gentle rise a short distance behind him where they sat in silence regarding him intently.

Usha, the wind, who carries scent, also carries sound. Today, Usha carried both the scent and the sound of the *shiftas* away from the keen nostrils and the ears of the apeman. Perhaps, endowed as he was with supersensitive perceptive faculties, Tarzan should have sensed the presence of an enemy; but "Even the worthy Homer sometimes nods."

However self-sufficient an animal may be it is endowed with caution, for there is none that has not its enemies. The weaker herbivora must be always on the alert for the lion, the leopard, and man; the elephant, the rhinoceros, and the lion may never relax their vigilance against man; and man must always be on guard against these and others. Yet one may not say that such caution connotes either fear or cowardice; for Tarzan, who was without fear, was the personification of caution, especially when he was far from his own stamping grounds as he was today and every creature a potential enemy.

The combination of ravenous hunger with the opportunity to satisfy it may have placed caution in abeyance as, oftentimes, a certain recklessness born of pride in his might did; but, be that as it may, the fact remains that Tarzan was wholly ignorant of the presence of that little knot of villainous bandits who were quite prepared to kill him, or anyone else, for a few poor weapons or for nothing at all.

The circumstances that brought Tarzan northward into Kaffa are not a part of this story. Perhaps they were not urgent, for the Lord of the Jungle loves to roam remote fastnesses still unspoiled by the devastating hand of civilization and needs but trifling incentive to do so. Still unsated with adventure, it may be that Abyssinia's three hundred fifty thousand square miles of semisavagery held an irresistible lure for him in their suggestion of mysterious back country and in the ethnological secrets they have guarded from time immemorial.

Wanderer, adventurer, outcast, Greek phalanx, and Roman legion, all have entered Abyssinia within times chronicled in history or legend never to reappear; and it is even believed by some that she holds the secret of the lost tribes of Israel. What wonders, then, what adventures, might not her remote corners reveal!

At the moment, however, Tarzan's mind was not occupied by thoughts of adventure; he did not know that it loomed threateningly behind him; his concern and his interest were centered upon the buck which he intended should satisfy the craving of his ravenous hunger. He crept cautiously forward. Than he, not even Sheeta, the leopard, stalks more silently or more stealthily.

From behind, the white-robed *shiftas* moved from the little rise where they had been watching him in silence, moved down toward him with spear and long-barreled matchlock. They were puzzled. Never before had they seen a white man like this one; but if curiosity were in their minds, there was only murder in their hearts.

The buck raised his head occasionally to glance about him, wary, suspicious; and when he did so, Tarzan froze into immobility. Suddenly the animal's gaze centered for an instant upon something in the direction of the ape-man; then it wheeled and bounded away. Instantly Tarzan glanced behind him, for he knew that it had not been he who had frightened his quarry but something beyond and behind him that the alert eyes of Wappi had discovered; and that quick glance revealed a half dozen horsemen moving slowly toward him, told him what they were, and explained their purpose; for, knowing that they were *shiftas*, he knew that they came only to rob and kill—knew that here were enemies more ruthless than Numa.

When they saw that he had discovered them, the horsemen broke into a gallop and bore down upon him, waving their weapons and shouting. They did not fire, evidently holding in contempt this primitively armed victim, but seemed to purpose riding him down and trampling him beneath the hoofs of their horses or impaling him upon their spears. Perhaps they thought that he would seek safety in flight, thereby giving them the added thrill of the chase; and what quarry could give the hunter greater thrills than man!

But Tarzan did not turn and run. He knew every possible avenue of escape within the radius of his vision for every danger that might reasonably be expected to confront him here, for it is the business of the creatures of the wild to know these things if they are to survive; and so he knew that there was no escape from mounted men by flight. But this knowledge threw him into no panic. Could the requirements of self-preservation have been best achieved by flight, he would have fled; but as they could not, he adopted the alternative quite as a matter of course—he stood to fight, ready to seize upon any fortuitous circumstance that might offer a chance of escape.

Tall, magnificently proportioned, muscled more like Apollo than like Hercules, garbed only in a narrow G string of lion skin with a lion's tail depending before and behind, he presented a splendid figure of primitive manhood that suggested more, perhaps, the demigod of the forest than it did man. Across his back hung his quiver of arrows and a light, short spear; the loose coils of his grass rope lay across one bronzed shoulder; at his hip swung the hunting knife of his father, the knife that had given the boy-Tarzan the first suggestion of his coming supremacy over the other beasts of the jungle on that far gone day when his youthful hand drove it into the heart of Bolgani, the gorilla; in his left hand was his bow and between the fingers four extra arrows.

As Ara, the lightning, so is Tarzan for swiftness. The instant that he had discovered and recognized the menace creeping upon him from behind and known that he had been seen by the horsemen he had leaped to his feet, and in the same instant strung his bow. Now, perhaps even before the leading *shiftas* realized the danger that confronted them, the bow was bent, the shaft sped.

Short but powerful was the bow of the ape-man; short, that it might be easily carried through the forest and the jungle; powerful, that it might send its shafts through the toughest hide to a vital organ of its prey. Such a bow was this that no ordinary man might bend it.

Straight through the heart of the leading *shifta* drove the first arrow, and as the fellow threw his arms above his head and lunged from his saddle four more arrows sped with lightning-like rapidity from the bow of the ape-man, and every arrow found a target. Another *shifta* dropped to ride no more, and three were wounded.

Only seconds had elapsed since Tarzan had discovered his danger, and already the four remaining horsemen were upon him. The three who were wounded were more interested in the feathered shafts protruding from their bodies than in the quarry they had expected so easily to overcome; but the fourth was whole, and he thundered down upon the ape-man with his spear set for the great bronzed chest.

There could be no retreat for Tarzan; there could be no side-stepping to avoid the thrust, for a step to either side would have carried him in front of one of the other horsemen. He had but a single slender hope for survival, and that hope, forlorn though it appeared, he seized upon with the celerity, strength, and agility that make Tarzan Tarzan. Slipping his bowstring about his neck after his final shot, he struck up the point of the menacing weapon of his antagonist, and grasping the man's arm swung himself to the horse's back behind the rider.

As steel-thewed fingers closed upon the *shifta's* throat he voiced a single piercing scream; then a knife drove home beneath his left shoulder blade, and Tarzan hurled the body from the saddle. The terrified horse, running free with flying reins, tore through the bushes and the reeds into the river, while the remaining *shiftas*, disabled by their wounds, were glad to abandon the chase upon the bank, though one of them, retaining more vitality than his companions, did raise his matchlock and send a parting shot after the escaping quarry.

The river was a narrow, sluggish stream but deep in the channel; and as the horse plunged into it, Tarzan saw a commotion in the water a few yards downstream and then the outline of a long, sinuous body moving swiftly toward them. It was Gimla, the crocodile. The horse saw it too and, becoming frantic, turned upstream in an effort to escape. Tarzan climbed over the high cantle of the Abyssinian saddle and unslung his spear in the rather futile hope of holding the reptile at bay until his mount could reach the safety of the opposite bank toward which he was now attempting to guide him.

Gimla is as swift as he is voracious. He was already at the horse's rump, with opened jaws, when the *shifta* at the river's edge fired wildly at the ape-man. It was well for Tarzan that the wounded man had fired hurriedly; for simultaneously with the report of the firearm, the crocodile dove; and the frenzied lashing of the water about him evidenced the fact that he had been mortally wounded.

A moment later the horse that Tarzan rode reached the opposite bank and clambered to the safety of dry land. Now he was under control again; and the ape-man wheeled him about and sent a parting arrow across the river toward the angry, cursing bandits upon the opposite side, an arrow that found its mark in the thigh of the already wounded man who had unwittingly rescued Tarzan from a serious situation with the shot that had been intended to kill him.

To the accompaniment of a few wild and scattered shots, Tarzan of the Apes galloped toward a nearby forest into which he disappeared from the sight of the angry *shiftas*.

2

The White Prisoner

F AR to the south a lion rose from his kill and walked
majestically to the edge of a nearby river. He cast not
so much as a single glance at the circle of hyenas and
jackals that had ringed him and his kill waiting for him
to depart and which had broken and retreated as he rose.
Nor, when the hyenas rushed in to tear at what he had left,
did he appear even to see them.

There were the pride and bearing of royalty in the mien of
this mighty beast; and to add to his impressiveness were his
great size, his yellow, almost golden, coat, and his great black
mane. When he had drunk his fill, he lifted his massive head
and voiced a roar, as is the habit of lions when they have
fed and drunk; and the earth shook to his thunderous voice,
and a hush fell upon the jungle.

Now he should have sought his lair and slept, to go forth
again at night and kill; but he did not do so. He did not do
at all what might have been expected of a lion under similar
circumstances. He raised his head and sniffed the air, and
then he put his nose to the ground and moved to and fro
like a hunting dog searching for a game scent. Finally he
halted and voiced a low roar; then, with head raised, he
moved off along a trail that led toward the north. The
hyenas were glad to see him go; so were the jackals, who
wished that the hyenas would go also. Ska, the vulture,
circling above, wished that they would all leave.

At about the same time, many marches to the north, three
angry, wounded *shiftas* viewed their dead comrades and

cursed the fate that had led them upon the trail of the strange white giant; then they stripped the clothing and weapons from their dead fellows and rode away, loudly vowing vengeance should they ever again come upon the author of their discomfiture and secretly hoping that they never would. They hoped that they were done with him, but they were not.

Shortly after he had entered the forest, Tarzan swung to an overhanging branch beneath which his mount was passing and let the animal go its way. The ape-man was angry; the *shiftas* had frightened away his dinner. That they had sought to kill him annoyed him far less than the fact that they had spoiled his hunting. Now he must commence his search for meat all over again, but when he had filled his belly he would look into this matter of *shiftas*. Of this he was certain.

Tarzan had considered the gastronomic potentialities of the bandit's horse, but had discarded the idea. On several occasions in the past he had been forced to eat horse meat, but he had not liked it. Although he was hungry, he was far from famished; and so he preferred to hunt again until he found flesh more palatable, nor was it long before he had made his kill and eaten.

Satisfied, he lay up for a while in the crotch of a tree, but not for long. His active mind was considering the matter of the *shiftas*. Here was something that should be looked into. If the band were on the march, he need not concern himself about them; but if they were permanently located in this district, that was a different matter; for Tarzan expected to be here for some time; and it was well to know the nature, the number, and the location of all enemies. Furthermore, he felt that he could not let them escape without some additional punishment for the inconvenience they had caused him.

Returning to the river, Tarzan crossed it and took up the plain trail of the *shiftas*. It led him up and down across some low hills and then down into the narrow valley of the stream that he had crossed farther up. Here the floor of the valley was forested, the river winding through the wood. Into this wood the trail led.

It was almost dark now; the brief equatorial twilight was rapidly fading into the night; the nocturnal life of the forest and the hills was awakening; from down among the deepening shadows of the valley came the coughing grunts of a hunting lion. Tarzan sniffed the warm air rising from the valley toward the mountains; it carried with it the odors of a camp and the scent spoor of man. He raised his head, and from his deep chest rumbled a full-throated roar. Tarzan of the Apes was hunting too.

In the gathering shadows he stood then erect and silent, a lonely figure standing in solitary grandeur upon that desolate hillside. Swiftly the silent night enveloped him; his figure merged with the darkness that made hill and valley, river and forest one. Not until then did Tarzan move; then he stepped down on silent feet toward the forest. Now was every sense alert, for now the great cats would be hunting. Often his sensitive nostrils quivered as they searched the air; no slightest sound escaped his keen ears.

As he advanced, the man scent became stronger, guiding his steps. Nearer and nearer sounded the deep cough of the lion; but of Numa Tarzan had little fear at present, knowing that the great cat, being up wind, could not be aware of his presence. Doubtless Numa had heard the ape-man's roar, but he could not know that its author was approaching him.

Tarzan had estimated the lion's distance down the valley and the distance that lay between himself and the forest and had guessed that he would reach the trees before their paths crossed. He was not hunting for Numa, the lion, and with the natural caution of the wild beasts, he would avoid an encounter. It was not food either that he hunted, for his belly was full, but man, the archenemy of all created things.

It was difficult for Tarzan to think of himself as a man, and his psychology was more often that of the wild beast than the human, nor was he particularly proud of his species. While he appreciated the intellectual superiority of man over other creatures, he harbored contempt for him because he had wasted the greater part of his inheritance. To Tarzan, as to many other created things, contentment is the highest ultimate goal of achievement, and health and culture the principal avenues along which man may approach this goal. With scorn the ape-man viewed the overwhelming majority of mankind which was wanting in either one essential or the other, when not wanting in both. He saw the greed, the selfishness, the cowardice, and the cruelty of man; and, in view of man's vaunted mentality, he knew that these characteristics placed man upon a lower spiritual scale than the beasts, while barring him eternally from the goal of contentment.

So now, as he sought the lair of the man-things, it was not in the spirit of one who seeks his own kind but of a beast which reconnoiters the position of an enemy. The mingled odors of a camp grew stronger in his nostrils, the scents of horses and men and food and smoke. To you or to me, alone in a savage wilderness, engulfed in darkness, cognizant of the near approach of a hunting lion, these odors would have been most welcome; but Tarzan's reaction to them was that of the wild beast that knows man only as an enemy—his snarling muscles tensed as he smothered a low growl.

As Tarzan reached the edge of the forest the lion was but a short distance to his right and approaching; so the ape-man took to the trees, through which he swung silently toward the camp of the *shiftas*. Numa heard him then and roared, and the men in the camp threw more wood upon the beast fire.

To a tree overlooking the camp, Tarzan made his way. Below him he saw a band of some twenty men with their horses and equipment. A rude boma of branches and brush had been erected about the camp site as a partial protection against wild beasts, but more dependence was evidently placed upon the fire which they kept burning in the center of the camp.

In a single quick glance the ape-man took in the details of the scene below him, and then his eyes came to rest upon the only one that aroused either interest or curiosity, a white man who lay securely bound a short distance from the fire.

Ordinarily, Tarzan was no more concerned by the fate of a white man than by that of a black man or any other created thing to which he was not bound by ties of friendship; the life of a man meant less to Tarzan of the Apes than the life of an ape. But in this instance there were two factors that made the life of the captive a matter of interest to the lord of the jungle. First, and probably predominant, was his desire to be further avenged upon the *shiftas* for their wanton attack upon him, which had frightened away his intended kill; the second was curiosity, for the white man that lay bound below him was different from any that he had seen before, at least in so far as his apparel was concerned.

His only garment appeared to be a habergeon made up of ivory discs that partially overlay one another, unless certain ankle, wrist, neck, and head ornaments might have been considered to possess such utilitarian properties as to entitle them to a similar classification. Except for these, his arms and legs were naked. His head rested upon the ground with the face turned away from Tarzan so that the ape-man could not see his features but only that his hair was heavy and black.

As he watched the camp, seeking for some suggestion as to how he might most annoy or inconvenience the bandits, it occurred to Tarzan that a just reprisal would consist in taking from them something that they wanted, just as they had deprived him of the buck he had desired. Evidently they wished the prisoner very much or they would not have gone to the trouble of securing him so carefully; so this fact decided Tarzan to steal the white man from them. Perhaps curiosity also had a considerable part in inducing this decision, for the strange apparel of the prisoner had aroused within the ape-man a desire to know more concerning him.

To accomplish his design, he decided to wait until the camp slept; and settling himself comfortably in a crotch of the tree, he prepared to keep his vigil with the tireless patience of the hunting beast he was. As he watched, he saw several of the *shiftas* attempt to communicate with their prisoner; but it was evident that neither understood the other.

Tarzan was familiar with the language spoken by the Kafichos and Gallas, and the questions that they put to their prisoner aroused his curiosity still further. There was one question that they asked him in many different ways, in several dialects, and in signs which the captive either did not understand or pretended not to. Tarzan was inclined to believe that the latter was true, for the sign language was such that it could scarcely be misunderstood. They were asking him the way to a place where there was much ivory and gold, but they got no information from him.

"The pig understands us well enough," growled one of the *shiftas;* "he is just pretending that he does not."

"If he won't tell us, what is the use of carrying him around with us and feeding him?" demanded another. "We might as well kill him now."

"We will let him think it over tonight," replied one who was evidently the leader, "and if he still refuses to speak in the morning, we will kill him then."

This decision they attempted to transmit to the prisoner both by words and signs, and then they squatted about the fire and discussed the occurrences of the day and their plans for the future. The principal topic of their conversation was the strange white giant who had slain three of their number and escaped upon one of their horses; and after this had been debated thoroughly and in detail for some time, and the three survivors of the encounter had boasted severally of their deeds of valor, they withdrew to the rude shelters they had constructed and left the night to Tarzan, Numa, and a single sentry.

The silent watcher among the shadows of the tree waited on in patience until the camp should be sunk in deepest slumber and, waiting, planned the stroke that was to rob the *shiftas* of their prey and satisfy his own desire for revenge. As he patiently bided his time, there came strongly to his nostrils the scent spoor of Numa, the lion; and he guessed that the carnivore, attracted by the presence of the horses, was coming to investigate the camp. That he would enter it, he doubted, for the sentry was keeping the fire blazing brightly; and Numa seldom dares the fearful mystery of flames unless goaded by extreme hunger.

At last the ape-man felt that the time had come when he might translate his plan into action; all but the sentry were wrapped in slumber, and even he was dozing beside the fire. As noiselessly as the shadow of a shadow Tarzan descended from the tree, keeping well in the shadow cast by the beast fire.

For a moment he stood in silence, listening. He heard the breathing of Numa in the darkness beyond the circle of firelight, and knew that the king of beasts was near and watching. Then he looked from behind the great bole of the tree and saw that the sentry's back was still turned toward him. Silently he moved into the open; stealthily, on soundless feet, he crept toward the unsuspecting bandit. He saw the matchlock across the fellow's knees; and for it he had respect, as have all jungle animals that have been hunted.

Closer and closer he came to his prey. At last he crouched directly behind him. There must be no noise, no outcry. Tarzan waited. Beyond the rim of fire waited Numa, expectant, for he saw that very gradually the flames were diminishing. A bronzed hand shot quickly forward, fingers of steel gripped the brown throat of the sentry almost at the instant that a knife was driven from below his left shoulder blade into his heart. The sentry was dead without knowing that death threatened him, a merciful ending.

Tarzan withdrew the knife from the limp body and wiped the blade upon the once white robe of his victim; then he moved softly toward the prisoner who was lying in the open. For him, they had not bothered to build a shelter. As he made his way toward the man, Tarzan passed close to two of the shelters in which lay members of the band; but he made no noise that might awaken them. When he approached the captive more closely, he saw in the diminishing light of the fire that the man's eyes were open and that he was regarding Tarzan with level, though questioning, gaze. The ape-man put a finger to his lips to enjoin silence, and then he came and knelt beside the man and cut the thongs that secured his wrists and ankles; then he helped him to his feet, for the thongs had been drawn tightly, and his legs were numb.

For a moment he waited while the stranger tested his feet and moved them rapidly in an effort to restore circulation; then he beckoned him to follow, and all would have been well but for Numa, the lion. At this moment, either to voice his anger against the flames or to terrify the horses into a stampede, he elected to voice a thunderous roar.

So close was the lion that the sudden shattering of the deep silence of the night startled every sleeper to wakefulness. A dozen men seized their matchlocks and leaped from their shelters. In the waning light of the fire they saw no lion; but they saw their liberated captive, and they saw Tarzan of the Apes standing beside him.

Among those who ran from the shelters was the least seriously wounded of Tarzan's victims of the afternoon. Instantly recognizing the bronzed white giant, he shouted loudly to his companions, "It is he! It is the white demon who killed our friends today."

"Kill him!" screamed another.

"Kill them both!" cried the leader of the *shiftas*.

Completely surrounding the two white men, the *shiftas* advanced upon them; but they dared not fire because of fear that they might wound one of their own comrades. Nor could Tarzan loose an arrow nor cast a spear, for he had left all his weapons except his rope and his knife hidden in the tree above the camp that he might move with the utmost freedom and in silence while seeking to liberate the captive.

One of the bandits, more courageous, probably because less intelligent, than his fellows, rushed to close quarters with musket clubbed. It was his undoing. The man-beast crouched, growling; and, as the other was almost upon him, charged. The musket butt, hurtling through the air to strike him down, he dodged; and then he seized the weapon and wrenched it from the *shifta's* grasp as though it had been a toy in a child's hands.

Tossing the matchlock at the feet of his companion, Tarzan laid hold upon the rash Galla, spun him around, and held him as a shield against the weapons of his fellows. But despite this reverse the other *shiftas* gave no indication of giving up the battle. They saw before them two men practically defenseless, and now with redoubled shouts they pushed closer.

Two of them rushed in behind the ape-man, for it was he they feared the more; but they were to learn that their former prisoner might not be considered lightly. He had picked up the musket that Tarzan had cast aside and, grasping it close to the muzzle, was using it as a club. The heavy butt struck the foremost bandit heavily upon the side of the head, dropping him like a felled ox; and as it swung again, the second bandit leaped back barely in time to avoid a similar fate.

A quick backward glance assured Tarzan that his companion was proving himself a worthy ally, but it was evident that they could not hope to hold out long against the superior numbers pitted against them. Their only hope, he believed, lay in making a sudden, concerted rush through the thin line of foemen surrounding them, and he sought to convey his plan to the man standing back to back with him; but though he spoke to him in English and in the several continental languages with which the ape-man was familiar the only reply he received was in a language that he himself had never before heard.

What was he to do? They must go together, and both must understand the purpose animating Tarzan. But how was that possible if they could not communicate with one another? Tarzan turned and touched the other lightly on the shoulder; then he jerked his thumb in the direction he intended going and beckoned with a nod of his head.

Instantly the man nodded his understanding and wheeled about as Tarzan started to charge, still bearing the struggling *shifta* in his grasp; but the *shiftas* were determined not to let these two escape; and while they could not fire for fear of killing their comrade, they stood their ground with clubbed muskets and with spears; so that the outcome looked dark indeed for the lord of the jungle and his companion.

Using the man in his grasp as a flail, Tarzan sought to mow down those standing between him and liberty; but there were many of them, and presently they succeeded in dragging their comrade from the clutches of the ape-man. Now it seemed that the situation of the two whites was hopeless, for there was no longer anything to prevent the bandits using their matchlocks to advantage. The *shiftas* were in such a transport of rage that nothing less than the extermination of these two foes would satisfy them; but Tarzan and the other pressed on so closely that the muskets were useless against them for the moment; though presently some of the *shiftas* withdrew a little to one side where they might have free use of their weapons.

One fellow in particular was well placed to fire without endangering any of his fellows, and raising his matchlock to his shoulder he took careful aim at Tarzan.

3

Cats by Night

A S THE man raised his weapon to his shoulder to fire at Tarzan, a scream of warning burst from the lips of one of his comrades, to be drowned by the throaty roar of Numa, the lion, as the swift rush of his charge carried him over the boma into the midst of the camp.

The man who would have killed Tarzan cast a quick backward glance as the warning cry apprised him of his danger; and when he saw the lion he cast away his rifle in his excitement and terror, his terrified scream mingled with the voice of Numa, and in his anxiety to escape the fangs of the man-eater he rushed into the arms of the ape-man.

The lion, momentarily confused by the firelight and the swift movement and the shouts of the men, paused, crouching, as he looked to right and left. In that brief instant Tarzan seized the fleeing *shifta*, lifted him high above his head, and hurled him into the face of Numa; then, as the lion seized its prey and its great jaws closed upon the head and shoulder of the hapless bandit, he motioned to his companion to follow him, and, running directly past the lion, leaped the boma at the very point that Numa had leaped it. Close at his heels was the white captive of the *shiftas*, and before the bandits had recovered from the first shock and surprise of the lion's unexpected charge the two had disappeared in the shadows of the night.

Just outside the camp Tarzan left his companion for a moment while he swung into the tree where he had left his weapons and recovered them; then he led the way out of the valley up into the hills. At his elbow trotted the silent white man he had rescued from certain death at the hands of the Kaficho and Galla bandits.

During the brief encounter in the camp Tarzan had noted with admiration the strength, agility, and courage of the stranger who had aroused both his interest and his curiosity. Here, seemingly, was a man moulded to the dimensions of Tarzan's own standards, a quiet, resourceful, courageous fighting man. Radiating that intangible aura which we call personality, even in his silences he impressed the ape-man with a conviction that loyalty and dependability were innate characteristics of the man; so Tarzan, who ordinarily preferred to be alone, was not displeased to have the companionship of this stranger.

The moon, almost full, had risen above the black mountain mass to the east, shedding her soft light on hill and valley and forest, transforming the scene once more into that of a new world which was different from the world of daylight and from the world of moonless night, a world of strange greys and silvery greens.

Up toward a fringe of forest that clothed the upper slopes of the foothills and dipped down into canyon and ravine the two men moved as noiselessly as the passing shadow of a cloud, yet to one hidden in the dark recesses of the wood above, their approach was not unheralded, for on the breath of Usha, the wind, it was borne ahead of them to the cunning nostrils of the prince of hunters.

Sheeta, the panther, was hungry. For several days prey had been scarce and elusive. Now, in his nostrils, the scent of the man-things grew stronger as they drew nearer. It was the pure scent of man that came to him unvitiated by the hated odor of the flame-belching thunder stick that he feared and hated. Eagerly, Sheeta, the panther, awaited the coming of the men.

Within the forest, Tarzan sought a tree where they might lie up for the night. He had eaten and was not hungry. Whether or not his companion had eaten was his own concern. This was a law of the jungle from which Tarzan might deviate for a weak or wounded companion but not for a strong man able to provide for himself. Had he killed, he would have shared his kill; but he would not go forth and hunt for another.

Tarzan found a branch that forked horizontally. With his hunting knife he cut other branches and laid them across the two arms of the Y thus formed. Over this rude platform he spread leaves; and then he lay down to sleep, while from an adjacent tree up wind Sheeta watched him. Sheeta also watched the other man-thing on the ground between the two trees. The great cat did not move; he seemed scarcely to breathe. Even Tarzan was unaware of his presence, yet the ape-man was restless. A sense so delicate that he was not objectively aware of its existence seemed to warn him that all was not well. He listened intently and sniffed the air but detected nothing amiss. Below him, his companion was making his bed upon the ground in preference to risking the high-flung branches of the trees to which he was unaccustomed. It was the man upon the ground that Sheeta watched.

At last, his bed of leaves and grasses arranged to suit him, Tarzan's companion lay down. Sheeta waited. Gradually, almost imperceptibly, the sinuous muscles were drawing the hind quarters forward beneath the sleek body in preparation for the spring. Sheeta edged forward on the great limb upon which he crouched, but in doing so he caused the branch to move slightly and the leaves at its end to rustle just a little. Your ears or mine would not have been conscious of any noise, but the ears of Tarzan are not as are yours or mine.

He heard; and his eyes, turning quickly, sought and found the intruder. At the same instant Sheeta launched himself at the man lying on his rude pallet on the ground below; and as Sheeta sprang so did Tarzan. What happened happened very quickly; it was a matter of seconds only.

As the two beasts sprang, Tarzan voiced a roar that was intended both to warn his companion and to distract the attention of Sheeta from his prey. The man upon the ground leaped quickly to one side, prompted more by an instinctive reaction than by reason. The panther's body brushed him as it struck the ground, but the beast's thoughts were now upon the thing that had voiced that menacing roar rather than upon its intended prey.

Wheeling as he leaped aside, the man turned and saw the savage carnivore just as Tarzan landed full upon the beast's back. He heard the mingled growls of the two as they closed in battle, and his scalp stiffened as he realized that the sounds coming from the lips of his companion were quite as bestial as those issuing from the throat of the carnivore.

Tarzan sought a hold about the neck of the panther, while the great cat instantly attempted to roll over on its back that it might rip the body of its antagonist to shreds with the terrible talons that armed its hind feet. But this strategy the ape-man had anticipated; and rolling beneath Sheeta as Sheeta rolled, he locked his powerful legs beneath the belly of the panther; then the great cat leaped to its feet again and sought to shake the man-thing from its back; and all the while a mighty arm was tightening about its neck, closing off its wind.

With frantic leaps and bounds the panther hurled itself about in the moonlight while Tarzan's companion stood unarmed and helpless. Twice he had tried to run in and assist the ape-man, but both times the two bodies had struck him and sent him spinning across the ground. Now he saw a new factor being injected into the battle; Tarzan had succeeded in drawing his knife. Momentarily the blade flashed before his eyes; then it was buried in the body of Sheeta. The cat, screaming from pain and rage, redoubled its efforts to dislodge the creature clinging to it in the embrace of death; but again the knife fell.

Now Sheeta stood trembling upon uncertain feet as once again the knife was plunged deeply into his side; then, his great voice forever stilled, he sank lifeless to the ground as the ape-man rolled from beneath him and sprang to his feet.

The man whose life Tarzan had saved came forward and laid a hand upon the shoulder of the ape-man, speaking a few words in a low voice but in a tongue that Tarzan did not understand though he guessed that it expressed the gratitude that the manner of the man betokened.

What thoughts were in the mind of Tarzan's companion? Twice within an hour this strange white man had saved him from death. For what reasons, the man could not guess. That sentiments of friendship and loyalty were aroused in his breast would seem only natural if he possessed either honor or gratitude, but of this we can have no knowledge until we know him better. As yet he is not even a name to

us; and, following the policy of Tarzan, we shall not judge
him until we know him better; then we may learn to like
him, or we may have reason to despise him.

Influenced by the attack of the panther and knowing that
Numa was abroad, Tarzan, by signs, persuaded the man to
come up into the tree; and here the ape-man helped him
construct a nest similar to his own. For the balance of the
night they slept in peace, and the sun was an hour old before either stirred the following morning; then the ape-man
rose and stretched himself.

Nearby, the other man sat up and looked about him.
His eyes met Tarzan's, and he smiled and nodded. For the
first time the ape-man had an opportunity to examine his
new acquaintance by daylight. The man had removed his
single garment for the night, covering himself with leaves
and branches. Now as he arose, his only garment was a G
string, and Tarzan saw six feet of well-muscled, well-propor-
tioned body topped by a head that seemed to bespeak breeding and intelligence. The man's features were strong, clear
cut, and harmoniously placed; the face was more noticeable
for strength and rugged masculinity than for beauty.

The wild beast in Tarzan looked into the brown eyes of
the stranger and was satisfied that here was one who might
be trusted; the man in him noted the headband that confined the black hair, saw the strangely wrought ivory ornament in the center of the forehead, the habergeon that he
was now donning, the ivory ornaments on wrists and ankles,
and found his curiosity piqued.

The ivory ornament in the center of the headband was
shaped like a concave, curved trowel, the point of which
projected above the top of the man's head and curved forward. His wristlets and anklets were of long flat strips of
ivory laid close together and fastened around the limbs by
leather thongs that were laced through holes piercing the
strips near their tops and bottoms. His sandals were of
heavy leather, apparently elephant hide, and were supported
by leather thongs fastened to the bottoms of his anklets.

On each arm below the shoulder he wore an ivory disc
upon which was carved a design; about his neck was a band
of smaller ivory discs elaborately carved, and from the low-
est of these a strap ran down to his habergeon, which was
also supported by shoulder straps. Depending from each

side of his headband was another ivory disc of large size,
above which was a smaller disc. The larger discs covered
his ears. Heavy, curved, wedge-shaped pieces of ivory were
held, one upon each shoulder, by the same straps that supported his habergeon.

That all these trappings were solely for purposes of orna-
mentation Tarzan did not believe. He saw that almost without exception they would serve as a protection against a cut-
ting weapon such as a sword or battle-ax; and he could not
but wonder where the stalwart warrior who wore them had
had his genesis, for nowhere in the world, so far as Tarzan
knew, was there a race of men wearing armor and ornaments such as these.

But speculation concerning this matter was relegated to
the background of his thoughts by hunger and recollection
of the remains of yesterday's kill that he had hung high in
a tree of the forest farther up the river; so he dropped lightly to the ground, motioning the young warrior to follow
him; and set off in the direction of his cache, keeping his
keen senses always on the alert for enemies.

Cleverly hidden by leafy branches, the meat was intact
when Tarzan reached it. He cut several strips and tossed
them down to the warrior waiting on the ground below;
then he cut some for himself and crouching in a crotch proceeded to eat it raw. His companion watched him for a moment in surprise; then he made fire with a bit of steel and
flint and cooked his own portion.

As he ate, Tarzan's active mind was considering plans
for the future. He had come to Abyssinia for a specific purpose, though the matter was not of such immediate importance that it demanded instant attention. In fact, in the phi-
losophy that a lifetime of primitive environment had inspired, time was not an important consideration. The phe-
nomenon of this ivory-armored warrior aroused questions
that intrigued his interest to a far greater extent than did
the problems that had brought him thus far from his own
stamping grounds, and he decided that the latter should
wait the solving of the riddle of this seeming anachronism
that his new-made acquaintance presented.

Having no other means of communication than signs rendered an exchange of ideas between the two difficult, but
when they had finished their meal and Tarzan had descend-

ed to the ground he succeeded in asking his companion in what direction he wished to go. The warrior pointed in a northeasterly direction toward the high mountains; and, as plainly as he could through the medium of signs, invited Tarzan to accompany him to his country. This invitation Tarzan accepted and motioned the other to lead the way.

For days that stretched to weeks the two men struck deeper and deeper into the heart of a stupendous mountain system. Always mentally alert and eager to learn, Tarzan took advantage of the opportunity provided by time and propinquity to learn the language of his companion, and he proved such an apt pupil that they were soon able to make themselves understood to one another.

Among the first things that Tarzan learned was that his companion's name was Valthor, while Valthor took the earliest opportunity to evince an interest in the ape-man's weapons; and as he was unarmed, Tarzan spent a day in making a spear and bow and arrows for him. Thereafter, as Valthor taught the lord of the jungle to speak his language, Tarzan instructed the former in the use of the bow, the spear being already a familiar weapon to the young warrior.

Thus the days and the weeks passed and the two seemed no nearer the country of Valthor than when they had started from the vicinity of the camp of the *shiftas*. Tarzan found game of certain varieties plentiful in the mountains, and it was he who kept their larder supplied. The impressive scenery that was marked by rugged grandeur held the interest of the ape-man undiminished. He hunted, and he enjoyed the beauties of unspoiled nature, practically oblivious of the passage of time.

But Valthor was less patient; and at last, late one day when they found themselves at the head of a blind canyon where stupendous cliffs barred further progress, he admitted defeat. "I am lost," he said simply.

"That," remarked Tarzan, "I could have told you many days ago."

Valthor looked at him in surprise. "How could you know that," he demanded, "when you yourself do not know in what direction my country lies?"

"I know," replied the ape-man, "because during the past week you have led the way toward the four points of the compass, and today we are within five miles of where we were a week ago. Across this ridge at our right, not more than five miles away, is the little stream where I killed the ibex and the gnarled old tree in which we slept that night just seven suns ago."

Valthor scratched his head in perplexity, and then he smiled. "I cannot dispute you," he admitted. "Perhaps you are right, but what are we going to do?"

"Do you know in what direction your country lies from the camp in which I found you?" asked Tarzan.

"Thenar is due east of that point," replied Valthor; "of that I am positive."

"Then we are directly southwest of it now, for we have travelled a considerable distance toward the south since we entered the higher mountains. If your country lies in these mountains then it should not be difficult to find it if we can keep moving always in a northeasterly direction."

"This jumble of mountains with their twisting canyons and gorges confuses me," Valthor admitted. "You see, in all my life before I have never been farther from Thenar than the valley of Onthar, and both these valleys are surrounded by landmarks with which I am so familiar that I need no other guides. It has never been necessary for me to consult the positions of the sun, the moon, nor the stars before; and so they have been of no help to me since we set out in search of Thenar. Do you believe that you could hold a course toward the northeast in this maze of mountains? If you can, then you had better lead the way rather than I."

"I can go toward the northeast," Tarzan assured him, "but I cannot find your country unless it lies in my path."

"If we reach a point within fifty or a hundred miles of it, from some high eminence we shall see Xarator," explained Valthor; "and then I shall know my way to Thenar, for Xarator is almost due west of Athne."

"What are Xarator and Athne?" demanded Tarzan.

"Xarator is a great peak the center of which is filled with fire and molten rock. It lies at the north end of the valley of Onthar and belongs to the men of Cathne, the city of gold. Athne, the city of ivory, is the city from which I come. The men of Cathne, in the valley of Onthar, are the enemies of my people."

"Tomorrow, then," said Tarzan, "we shall set out for the city of Athne in the valley of Thenar."

As Tarzan and Valthor ate meat that they had cut from yesterday's kill and carried with them, many weary miles to the south a black-maned lion lashed his tail angrily and voiced a savage growl as he stood over the body of a buffalo calf he had killed and faced an angry bull pawing the earth and bellowing a few yards away.

Rare is the beast that will face Gorgo, the buffalo, when rage inflames his red-rimmed eyes; but the great lion showed no intention of leaving its prey even in the face of the bull's threatened charge. He stood his ground. The roars of the lion and the bull mingled in a savage, thunderous dissonance that shook the earth, stilling the voices of the lesser people of the jungle.

Gorgo gored the earth, working himself into a frenzy of rage. Behind him, bellowing, stood the mother of the slain calf. Perhaps she was urging her lord and master to avenge the murder. The other members of the herd had bolted into the thickest of the jungle leaving these two to contest with Numa his right to his kill, leaving vengeance to those powerful horns backed by that massive neck.

With a celerity and agility that belied his great weight, the bull charged. That two such huge beasts could move so quickly and so lightly seemed incredible, as it seemed incredible that any creature could either withstand or avoid the menace of those mighty horns; but the lion was ready, and as the bull was almost upon him, he leaped to one side, reared upon his hind feet and with one massive, taloned paw struck the bull a terrific blow on the side of its head that wheeled it half around and sent it stumbling to its knees, half stunned and bleeding, its great jawbone crushed and splintered. And before Gorgo could regain his feet, Numa leaped full upon his back, buried his teeth in the bulging muscles of the great neck, and with one paw reached for the nose of the bellowing bull, jerking the head back with a mighty surge that snapped the vertebrae.

Instantly the lion was on his feet again facing the cow, but she did not charge. Instead, bellowing, she crashed away into the jungle leaving the king of beasts standing with his forefeet upon his latest kill.

That night Numa fed well; yet when he had gorged himself he did not lie up as a lion should, but continued toward the north along the mysterious trail he had been following for many days.

4

Down the Flood

T HE new day dawned cloudy and threatening. The season of rains was over, but it appeared that a belated storm was gathering above the lofty peaks through which Tarzan and Valthor were searching for the elusive valley of Thenar. The chill of night was dissipated by no kindly warmth of sunlight. The two men shivered as they rose from their rude beds among the branches of a tree.

"We shall eat later," announced Tarzan, "after a little climbing has put warmth into our blood."

"If we are lucky enough to find anything to eat," rejoined Valthor.

"Tarzan seldom goes hungry," replied the ape-man. "He will not go hungry today. When Tarzan is ready to hunt, we shall eat."

Down the box canyon they went until Tarzan found a place where they might ascend the precipitous side wall; then they toiled upward, the warrior from Athne confident that each step would be his last as he clung to the steep face of the canyon wall but too proud to reveal his fear to the agile ape-man climbing so easily above him. But he did not fall, and at last the two stood upon the summit of a mighty ridge that led upward toward lofty peaks.

Valthor's heart was pounding and he was breathing heavily, but Tarzan showed no sign of exertion. He was about to continue on up the ridge, when he glanced at his companion and saw his condition; then he squatted on the ground with a laconic "Rest now"; and Valthor was glad to rest.

All day they moved toward the northeast. Sometimes it rained a little, and always it threatened to rain more. A great storm seemed always to be gathering, yet it never broke during the long day. Tarzan made a kill before noon, and they ate; but immediately afterward they started on again. The cold, damp, sunless air offered them no incentive for tarrying on the way.

It was late in the afternoon when they ascended out of a deep gorge and stood upon a lofty plateau. In the near foreground were no mountains, but at a distance lofty peaks were visible dimly through a light drizzle of rain. Suddenly Valthor voiced an exclamation of elation. "We have found it!" he cried. "There is Xarator!"

Tarzan looked in the direction that the other pointed and saw a mighty, flat-topped peak in the distance, directly above which low clouds were reflecting a dull red light. "So that is Xarator!" he remarked. "And Thenar is directly east of it?"

"Yes," replied Valthor; "which means that Onthar must be just below the edge of this plateau, almost directly in front of us. Come!"

The two walked quickly over the level, grassy ground for a mile or two to come at length to the edge of the plateau beyond which, and below them, stretched a wide valley.

"We are almost at the southern end of Onthar," said Valthor. "There is Cathne, the city of gold. See it—in the bend of the river at this end of that forest? It is a rich city, but its people are the enemies of my people."

Through the rain, Tarzan saw a walled city between a forest and a river. The houses were nearly all white, and there were many domes of dull yellow. The river, which ran between them and the city, was spanned by a bridge that was also a dull yellow color in the twilight of the late afternoon storm. Tarzan saw that the river extended the full length of the valley, a distance of fourteen or fifteen miles, being fed by smaller streams coming down out of the mountains. Also extending the length of the valley was what appeared to be a well-marked road. Near the center of the valley it branched, one fork following an affluent of the main stream with which it disappeared into the mouth of a canyon on the eastern side of the valley. Directly below them and extending to the northern extremity of Onthar was a level plain dotted with trees; across the river, a forest stretched from the farther bank to the steep hills that bounded Onthar on the east and southeast.

Tarzan's eyes wandered back to the city of Cathne. "Why do you call it the city of gold?" he asked.

"Do you not see the golden domes and the bridge of gold?" demanded Valthor.

"Are they covered with gold paint?" inquired Tarzan.

"They are covered with solid gold," replied Valthor. "The gold on some of the domes is an inch thick, and the bridge is built of solid blocks of gold."

Tarzan lifted his eyebrows. As he looked down upon this seemingly deserted and peaceful valley he could not but conjure another picture—a picture of what it would be if word of these vast riches were carried to the outside world, bringing the kindly beneficences of modern civilization and civilized men to Onthar. How the valley would hum and roar then with the sweet music of mill and factory! What a gorgeous spectacle would be painted against the African sky by tall chimneys spouting black smoke to hang like a sable curtain above the golden domes of Cathne!

"Where do they find their gold?" he asked.

"Their mines lie in the hills directly south of the city," replied Valthor.

"And where is your country, Thenar?" asked the ape-man.

"Just beyond the hills east of Onthar. Do you see where the river and the road cut through the forest about five miles above the city? You can see them entering the hills just beyond the forest."

"Yes," replied Tarzan; "I see."

"The road and the river run through the Pass of the Warriors into the valley of Thenar; a little northeast of the center of the valley lies Athne, the city of ivory; there, beyond the pass, is my country."

"How far are we from Athne?" inquired Tarzan.

"About twenty-five miles, possibly a little less," replied Valthor.

"We might as well start now, then," suggested the ape-man, "for in this rain it will be more comfortable to be on the march than to lie up until morning; and in your city we can find a dry place to sleep I presume."

"Certainly," replied Valthor, "but it will not be safe to attempt to cross Onthar by daylight. We should certainly be seen by the sentries on the gates of Cathne, and as these people are our enemies the chances are that we should never cross the valley without being either killed or taken prisoners. It will be bad enough at night on account of the lions, but by day it will be infinitely worse as we shall have both men and lions to contend with."

"What lions?" demanded Tarzan.

"The men of Cathne breed lions, and there are many at large in the valley," explained Valthor. "That great plain that you see below us, stretching the full length of the valley on this side of the river, is called the Field of the Lions. We shall be safer if we cross it after dark."

"Whatever you wish," agreed Tarzan with a shrug; "it is all the same to me if we start now or wait until dark."

"It is not very comfortable here," remarked the Athnean. "The rain is cold."

"I have been uncomfortable before," replied Tarzan; "rains do not last forever."

"If we were in Athne we should be very comfortable," sighed Valthor. "In my father's house there are fireplaces; even now the flames are roaring about great logs, and all is warmth and comfort."

"Above the clouds the sun is shining," replied Tarzan, "but we are not above the clouds; we are here where the sun is not shining and there is no fire, and we are cold." A faint smile touched his lips. "It does not warm me to speak of fires or the sun."

"Nevertheless, I wish I were in Athne," insisted Valthor. "It is a splendid city, and Thenar is a lovely valley. In Thenar we raise goats and sheep and elephants. In Thenar there are no lions except those that stray in from Onthar; those we kill. Our farmers raise vegetables and fruits and hay; our artizans manufacture leather goods; they make cloth from the hair of goats and the wool of sheep; our carvers work in ivory and wood.

"We trade a little with the outside world, paying for what we buy with ivory and gold. Were it not for the

Cathneans we should lead a happy, peaceful life without a care."

"What do you buy from the outside world, and of whom do you buy it?" asked Tarzan.

"We buy salt, of which we have none of our own," explained Valthor. "We also buy steel for our weapons and black slaves and occasionally a white woman, if she be young and pretty. These things we buy from a band of *shiftas*. With this same band we have traded since before the memory of man. *Shifta* chiefs and kings of Athne have come and gone, but our relations with this band have never altered. I was searching for them when I became lost and was captured by another band."

"Do you never trade with the people of Cathne?" asked the ape-man.

"Once each year there is a week's truce during which we trade with them in peace. They give us gold and foodstuffs and hay in exchange for the women, the salt, and the steel we buy from the *shiftas*, and the cloth, leather, and ivory that we produce.

"Besides mining gold, the Cathneans breed lions for war and sport, raise fruits, vegetables, cereals, and hay and work in gold and, to a lesser extent, in ivory. Their gold and their hay are the products most valuable to us; and of these we value the hay more, for without it we should have to decrease our elephant herds."

"Why should two peoples so dependent upon one another fight?" asked Tarzan.

Valthor shrugged. "I do not know; perhaps it is just a custom. Yet, though we talk much of wanting peace, we should miss the thrills and excitement that peace does not hold." His eyes brightened. "The raids!" he exclaimed. "There is a sport for men! The Cathneans come with their lions to hunt our goats, our sheep, our elephants, and us. They take heads for trophies, and above all they value the head of man. They try to take our women, and when they succeed then there is war, if the family of the woman seized be of sufficient importance.

"When we wish sport we go into Onthar after gold and women or just for the sport of killing men or capturing slaves. The greatest game of all is to sell a woman to a Cathnean for much gold and then take her away from him in a raid. No, I do not think that either we or the Cathneans would care for peace."

As Valthor talked, the invisible sun sank lower into the west; heavy clouds, dark and ominous, hid the peaks to the north, settling low over the upper end of the valley. "I think we may start now," he said; "it will soon be dark."

Downward through a gully, the sides of which hid them from the city of Cathne, the two men made their way toward the floor of the valley. From the heavy storm clouds burst a flash of lightning followed by the roar of thunder; upon the upper end of the valley the storm god loosed his wrath; water fell in a deluge of masses wiping from their sight the hills beyond the storm.

By the time they reached level ground the storm was upon them and the gully they had descended a raging mountain torrent. The swift night had fallen; utter darkness surrounded them, darkness frequently broken by vivid flashes of lightning. The pealing of the constant thunder was deafening. The rain engulfed them in solid sheets like the waves of the ocean. It was, perhaps, the most terrific storm that either of these men had ever seen.

They could not converse; only the lightning prevented their becoming separated, as it alone permitted Valthor to keep his course across the grassy floor of the valley in the direction of the city of gold where they would find the road that led to the Pass of the Warriors and on into the valley of Thenar.

Presently they came within sight of the lights of the city, a few dim lights framed by the casements of windows; and a moment later they were on the road and were moving northward against the full fury of the storm. And such a storm! As they moved toward its center it grew in intensity; against the wind that accompanied it they waged a grim battle that was sometimes to them and sometimes to the wind, for often it stopped them in their tracks and forced them back.

For miles they pitted their muscles against the Herculean strength of the storm god; and the rage of the storm god seemed to rise against them, knowing no bounds, as though he was furious that these two puny mortals should pit their strength against his. Suddenly, as though in a last titanic effort to overcome them, the lightning burst into a mighty blaze that illuminated the entire valley for seconds, the thunder crashed as it had never crashed before, and a mass of water fell that crushed the two men to earth.

As they staggered to their feet again foot-deep water swirled about their legs; they stood in a broad, racing torrent that rushed past them toward the river; but in that last effort the storm god had spent his force. The rain ceased; through a rift in the dark clouds the moon looked down, perhaps in wonder, upon a drowned world; and Valthor led the way again toward the Pass of the Warriors. The last storm of the rainy season was over.

It is seven miles from the Bridge of Gold, that is the gateway to the city of Cathne, to the ford where the road to Thenar crosses the river; and it required three hours for Valthor and Tarzan to cover the distance, two hours for the first third and one hour for the remainder; but at last they stood at the river's brink.

A boiling flood confronted them, tearing down a widened river toward the city of Cathne. Valthor hesitated. "Ordinarily," he said to Tarzan, "the water is little more than a foot deep. It must be three feet deep now."

"And it will soon be deeper," commented the ape-man. "Only a small portion of the storm waters have had time to reach this point from the hills and the upper valley. If we are going to cross tonight, we shall have to do it now."

"Very well," replied Valthor, "but follow me; I know the ford."

As the Athnean stepped into the water the clouds closed again beneath the moon and plunged the world once more into darkness. As Tarzan followed he could scarcely see his guide ahead of him; and as Valthor knew the ford he moved more rapidly than the ape-man with the result that presently Tarzan could not see him at all, but he felt his way toward the opposite bank without thought of disaster.

The force of the stream was mighty; but mighty, too, are the thews of Tarzan of the Apes. The water, which Valthor had thought to be three feet in depth, was soon surging to the ape-man's waist, and then he missed the ford and stepped into a hole. Instantly the current seized him and swept him away; not even the giant muscles of Tarzan could cope with the might of the flood.

The lord of the jungle fought the swirling waters in an effort to reach the opposite shore, but in their embrace he was powerless. Was the storm god proud or resentful to see one of his children succeed where he had failed? That is a difficult question to answer, for gods are strange creatures; they give to those who have and take from those who have not; they punish whom they love and are jealous and resentful; in which they resemble the creatures who conceived them.

Finding even his great strength powerless and weakening, Tarzan gave up the struggle to reach the opposite bank and devoted his efforts to keeping his nose above the surface of the angry flood. Even this was none too easy of accomplishment, as the rushing waters had a trick of twisting him about or turning him over. Often his head was submerged, and sometimes he floated feet first and sometimes head first; but he tried to rest his muscles as best he could against the time when some vagary of the torrent might carry him within reach of the bank upon one side or the other.

He knew that several miles below the city of Cathne the river entered a narrow gorge, for that he had seen from the edge of the plateau from which he had first viewed the valley of Onthar; and Valthor had told him that beyond the gorge it tumbled in a mighty falls a hundred feet to the bottom of a rocky canyon. Should he not succeed in escaping the clutches of the torrent before it carried him into the gorge his doom was sealed, but Tarzan felt neither fear nor panic. His life had been in jeopardy often during his savage existence, yet he still lived.

He wondered what had become of Valthor. Perhaps he, too, was being hurtled along either above or below him. But such was not the fact. Valthor had reached the opposite bank in safety and waited there for Tarzan. When the ape-man did not appear within a reasonable time, the Athnean shouted his name aloud; but though he received no answer he was still not sure that Tarzan was not upon the opposite side of the river, the loud roaring of which might have drowned the sound of the voice of either.

Then Valthor decided to wait until daylight, rather than abandon his friend in a country with which he was entirely unfamiliar. That the Athnean remained bespoke his loyalty as well as the high esteem in which he held the ape-man, for the dangers that might beset Tarzan in Onthar would prove even a greater menace to Valthor, an hereditary enemy of the Cathneans.

Through the long night he waited and, with the coming of dawn, eagerly scanned the opposite bank of the river, his slender hope for the safety of his friend dying when daylight failed to reveal any sign of him. Then, at last, he was convinced that Tarzan had been swept away to his death by the raging flood; and, with a heavy heart, he turned away from the river and resumed his interrupted journey toward the Pass of the Warriors and the Valley of Thenar.

5

The City of Gold

As Tarzan battled for his life in the swirling waters of the swollen river he lost all sense of time; the seemingly interminable struggle against death might have been enduring without beginning, might endure without end, in so far as his numbed senses were concerned. His efforts to delay the apparently inevitable end were now purely mechanical, instinctive reactions to the threat against self-preservation. The cold water had sapped the vitality of his mind as well as of his body, yet, while his heart beat, neither would admit defeat; subconsciously, without active volition, they sought to preserve him. It was well that they did.

Turnings in the river cast him occasionally against one shore and then the other. Always, then, his hands reached up in an attempt to grasp something that might stay his mad rush toward the falls and death; and at last success crowned their efforts—his fingers closed upon the stem of a heavy vine that trailed down the bank into the swirling waters, closed and held.

Instantly, almost miraculously, new life seemed to be instilled into the veins of the ape-man by the feel of that stout support in his grasp. Quickly he seized it with both hands; the river clutched at his body and tried to drag it onward toward its doom; but the vine held, and so did Tarzan.

Hand over hand the man dragged himself out of the water and onto the bank, where he lay for several minutes; then he rose slowly to his feet, shook himself like some great lion, and looked about him in the darkness, trying to penetrate the impenetrable night. Faintly, as through shrubbery, he thought that he saw a light shining dimly in the distance. Where there was a light, there should be men. Tarzan moved cautiously forward to investigate.

He knew that he had crossed the river but that he was a long distance from the point at which he had entered it. He wondered what had become of Valthor; and determined, after he had investigated the light, to start up the river in search of him; even though he feared that his companion had been swept away by the flood, as he had.

But a few steps from the river Tarzan encountered a wall, and when he was close to the wall he could no longer see the light. Reaching upward, he discovered that the top of the wall was still above the tips of his outstretched fingers; but walls which were made to keep one out also invited one to climb them. The ape-man, filled with the curiosity of the beast, desired now more than ever to investigate the light he had seen.

Stepping back a few paces, he ran toward the wall and sprang upward. His extended fingers gripped the top of the wall and clung there. Slowly he drew himself up, threw a leg across the capstones, and looked to see what might be seen upon the opposite side of the wall.

He did not see much; a square of dim light forty or fifty feet away; that was all, and it did not satisfy his curiosity. Silently he lowered himself to the ground upon the same side as the light and moved cautiously forward. Beneath his bare feet he felt stone flagging, and guessed that he was in a paved courtyard.

He had crossed about half the distance to the light when the retreating storm flashed a farewell bolt from the distance. This distant lightning but barely sufficed to momentarily relieve the darkness surrounding the ape-man, revealing a low building, a lighted window, a deeply recessed doorway in the shelter of which stood a man. It also revealed Tarzan to the man in the doorway.

Instantly the silence was shattered by the brazen clatter of a gong. The door swung open, and men bearing torches rushed out. Tarzan, impelled by the natural caution of the beast, turned to run; but as he did so, he saw other open doors upon his flanks; and armed men with torches were rushing from these as well.

Realizing that flight was useless, Tarzan stood still with folded arms as the men converged upon him from three directions. Perhaps his insatiate curiosity prompted him to await quietly the coming of the men as much as a realization of the futility of flight. Tarzan wanted to see what the men were like and what they would do. He knew that he must be in the city of gold, and his imagination was inflamed. If they threatened him, he could still fight; if they imprisoned him, he could escape; so, at least, thought Tarzan, whose self-confidence was in proportion to his great size and his giant strength.

The torches carried by some of the men showed Tarzan that he was in a paved, quad-rangular courtyard enclosed by buildings upon three sides and the wall he had scaled upon the fourth. Their light also revealed the fact that he was being surrounded by some fifty men armed with spears, the points of which were directed toward him in a menacing circle.

"Who are you?" demanded one of the men as the cordon drew tightly about him. The language in which the man spoke was the same as that which Tarzan had learned from Valthor, the common language of the enemy cities of Athne and Cathne.

"I am a stranger from a country far to the south," replied the ape-man.

"What are you doing inside the walls of the palace of Nemone?" The speaker's voice was threatening, his tone accusatory. Tarzan sensed that the presence of a stranger here was a crime in itself; but this made the situation all the more interesting; while the name, Nemone, possessed a quality that fired his interest.

"I was crossing the river far above here when the flood caught me and swept me down; it was only by chance that I finally made a landing here."

The man who had been questioning him shrugged. "Well," he admitted, "it is not for me to question you anyway. Come! You will have a chance to tell your story to an officer; but he will not believe it either."

As the men conducted Tarzan toward one of the buildings, he thought that they seemed more curious than hostile. It

was evident, however, that they were only common warriors without responsibility and that he might find the
attitude of the officer class entirely different.

They conducted him into a large, low-ceilinged room
which was furnished with rough benches and tables; upon
the walls hung weapons, spears and swords; and there were
shields of elephant hide studded with gold bosses. But there
were other things in this strange room that compelled the
interest of the ape-man far more than did the weapons and
the shields; upon the walls were mounted the heads of animals; there were the heads of sheep and goats and lions and
elephants. Among these, sinister and forbidding, were the
scowling heads of men. The sight of them reminded Tarzan
of the stories Valthor had told him of these men of Cathne.

Two men guarded Tarzan in one corner of the room, while
another was dispatched to notify a superior of the capture;
the remainder loafed about the room, talking, playing
games, cleaning their weapons. The prisoner took the opportunity to examine his captors.

They were well set up men, many of them not ill-
favored, though for the most part of ignorant and brutal
appearance. Their helmets, habergeons, wristlets, and anklets
were of elephant hide heavily embossed with gold studs.
Long hair from the manes of lions fringed the tops of their
anklets and wristlets and was also used for ornamental
purposes along the crests of their helmets and upon some of
their shields and weapons. The elephant hide that composed
their habergeons was cut into discs, and the habergeon
fabricated in a manner similar to that one of ivory which
Valthor had worn. In the center of each shield was a heavy
boss of solid gold. Upon the harnesses and weapons of
these common soldiers was a fortune in the precious
metal.

While Tarzan, immobile, silent, surveyed the scene with
eyes that seemed scarcely to move yet missed no detail,
two warriors entered the room; and the instant that they
crossed the threshold silence fell upon the men congregated in the chamber; and Tarzan knew by that these were
officers, though their trappings would have been sufficient
evidence of their superior stations in life.

Habergeons and helmets, wristlets and anklets were all of
gold and ivory, as were the hilts and scabbards of their

short, dagger-like swords. The two presented a gorgeous picture against the background of the grim room and the relatively somber trappings of the common soldiers.

At a word of command from one of the two, the common warriors fell back, clearing one end of the room; then the two seated themselves at a table and ordered Tarzan's guards to bring him forward. As the lord of the jungle halted before them both men surveyed him critically.

"Why are you in Onthar?" demanded one who was evidently the superior, since he propounded all the questions during the interview.

Tarzan answered this and other questions as he had answered similar ones at the time of his capture, but he sensed from the attitudes of the two officers that neither was impressed with the truth of his statements. They seemed to have preconceived a conviction concerning him that nothing which he might say could alter.

"He does not look much like an Athnean," remarked the younger man.

"That proves nothing," snapped the other. "Naked men look like naked men. He might pass for your own cousin were he garbed as you are garbed."

"Perhaps you are right, but why is he here? A man does not come alone from Thenar to raid in Onthar. Unless—" he hesitated; "unless he was sent to assassinate the Queen!"

"I had thought of that," said the older man. "Because of what happened to the last Athnean prisoners we took, the Athneans are very angry with the Queen. Yes, they might easily attempt to assassinate her."

"For what other reason would a stranger enter the palace grounds? He would know that he must die if he were caught."

"Of course, and this man expected to die; but he intended killing the Queen first. He was willing to martyr himself for Athne."

Tarzan was almost amused as he contemplated the ease with which these two convinced themselves that what they wanted to believe true, was true; but he realized that this form of one-sided trial might prove disastrous to him if his fate were to be decided by such a tribunal and so he was prompted to speak.

"I have never been in Athne," he said quietly. "I am from

a country far to the south. An accident brought me here. I am not an enemy. I have not come to kill your Queen or any other. Until today I did not know that your city existed." This was a long speech for Tarzan of the Apes. He was almost positive that it would not influence his captors, yet there was a chance that they might believe him. He wished to remain among these people until his curiosity concerning them had been satisfied, and he felt that he might only do this by winning their confidence; if they imprisoned him, he would see nothing while he was in prison; and when he got out of prison, he would see but little more; as he would then be concerned only with the business of escape.

Men are peculiar, and none knew this better than Tarzan, who, because he had seen rather less of men than of beasts, had been inclined to study those whom he had seen. Now he was studying the two men who were questioning him. The elder he judged to be a man accustomed to the exercise of great power; cunning, ruthless, cruel. Tarzan did not like him. His was the instinctive appraisal of the wild beast.

The younger man was of an entirely different mold. He was intelligent rather than cunning; his countenance bespoke a frank and open nature. The ape-man judged that he was both honest and courageous. It was true that he had agreed with all that the elder man had said, almost in contradiction of his own original statement that Tarzan did not resemble an Athnean; but in that the ape-man saw confirmation of his belief in the younger man's intelligence. Only a fool contradicts his superior for no good purpose.

While he was certain that the younger man had little authority, compared with that exercised by his superior, yet Tarzan thought best to address him rather than the other because he thought that he might win an ally in the younger man and was sure that he could never influence the elder unless it was very much to the latter's interests to be influenced. And so, when he spoke again, he spoke to the younger of the two officers.

"Are these men of Athne like me?" he asked.

For an instant the officer hesitated; then he said, quite frankly, "No; they are not like you. You are unlike any man that I have seen."

"Are their weapons like my weapons?" continued the

ape-man. "There are mine over in the corner of the room; your men took them away from me. Look at them."

Even the elder officer seemed interested. "Bring them here," he ordered one of the warriors.

The man brought them and laid them on the table before the two officers; the spear, the bow, the quiver of arrows, the grass rope, and the knife. The two men picked them up one by one and examined them carefully. Both seemed interested.

"Are they like the weapons of the Athneans?" demanded Tarzan. Of course he knew that they were not, but he thought it best not to acquaint these men with the fact that he had been consorting with one of their enemies.

"They are nothing like them," admitted the younger man. "What do you suppose this thing is for, Tomos?" he asked his companion as he examined Tarzan's bow.

"It may be a snare of some sort," replied Tomos; "probably for small animals—it would be useless against anything large."

"Let me take it," suggested Tarzan, "and I will show you how it is used."

The younger man handed the bow to the ape-man.

"Be careful, Gemnon," cautioned Tomos; "this may be a trick, a subterfuge by which he hopes to get possession of a weapon with which to kill us."

"He cannot kill us with that thing," replied Gemnon. "Let's see how he uses it. Go ahead— Let's see, what did you say your name is?"

"Tarzan," replied the lord of the jungle, "Tarzan of the Apes."

"Well, go ahead, Tarzan; but see that you don't attempt to attack any of us."

Tarzan stepped to the table and took an arrow from his quiver; then he glanced about the room. On the wall at the far end a lion's head with open mouth hung near the ceiling. With what appeared but a single swift motion he fitted the arrow to the bow, drew the feathered shaft to his shoulder, and released it.

Every eye in the room had been upon him, for the common warriors had been interested spectators of what had been transpiring; every eye saw the shaft quivering now where it protruded from the center of the lion's mouth;

and an involuntary exclamation broke from every throat, an exclamation in which were mingled surprise and applause.

"Take the thing away from him, Gemnon," snapped Tomos. "It is not a safe weapon in the hands of an enemy."

Tarzan tossed the bow to the table. "Do the Athneans use this weapon?" he asked.

Gemnon shook his head. "We know no men who use such a weapon," he replied.

"Then you must know that I am no Athnean," stated Tarzan, looking squarely at Tomos.

"It makes no difference where you are from," snapped Tomos; "you are an enemy."

The ape-man shrugged but remained silent. He had accomplished all that he had hoped for. He was sure that he had convinced them both that he was not an Athnean and had aroused the interest of the younger man, Gemnon. Something might come of this; though just what, he did not know himself.

Gemnon had leaned close to Tomos and was whispering in the latter's ear, evidently urging some action upon him. Tarzan could not hear what he was saying. The elder man listened impatiently; it was clear that he was not in accord with the suggestions of his junior.

"No," he said when the other had finished. "I will not permit anything of the sort. The life of the Queen is too sacred to risk by permitting this fellow any freedom. We shall lock him up for the night, and tomorrow decide what shall be done with him." He turned to a warrior who seemed to be an under-officer. "Take this fellow to the strong house," he said, "and see that he does not escape." Then he rose and strode from the room, followed by his younger companion.

When they had gone, the man in whose charge Tarzan had been left picked up the bow and examined it. "What do you call this thing?" he demanded.

"A bow," replied the ape-man.

"And these?"

"Arrows."

"Will they kill a man?"

"With them I have killed men and lions and buffaloes and elephants," replied Tarzan. "Would you like to learn how to se them?" Perhaps, he thought, a little kindly feeling in the uardroom might be helpful to him later on. Just at present e was not thinking of escape; these people and the city f gold were far too interesting to leave until he had seen more of them.

The man fingering the bow hesitated. Tarzan guessed that e wished to try his hand with the weapon but feared to lelay carrying out the order of his officer.

"It will take but a moment," suggested Tarzan. "See, let me how you."

Half reluctantly the man handed him the bow and Tarzan elected another arrow.

"Hold them like this," he directed and placed the bow nd arrow correctly in the other's hands. "Tell your men o stand aside; you may not shoot accurately at first. Aim at he lion's head, as I did. Now draw the bowstring back as ar as you can."

The man, of stocky, powerful build, tugged at the bow-tring; but the bow that Tarzan bent so easily he could carcely bend at all. When he released the arrow it flew but a few feet and dropped to the floor. "What's wrong?" he lemanded.

"It requires practice," the ape-man told him.

"There is a trick to it," insisted the under-officer. "Let me ee you do it again."

The other warriors, watching with manifest interest, whis-ered among themselves or commented openly. "It takes a trong man to bend that stick," said one.

"Althides is a strong man," retorted another.

"But he is not strong enough."

Althides, the under-officer, watched intently while Tarzan trung the bow again and bent it; he saw how easily the tranger flexed the heavy wood, and he marvelled. The other men looked on in open admiration, and this time a hout of approval arose as Tarzan's second arrow crowded the first in the mouth of the lion. When the symbols of high authority are absent men can be human.

Althides scratched his head. "I shall have to lock you up now," he said, "or old Tomos will have my head on the wall of his palace; but I shall practice with this strange weapon until I learn to use it. Are you sure that there is no trick in bending that thing you call a bow?"

"There is no trick to it," Tarzan assured him. "Make you self a lighter bow and you will find it easier, or bring me t material and I will make one for you."

"That I will do," exclaimed Althides. "Come now ar be locked up."

A guard accompanied Tarzan across the courtyard to an other building where he was placed in a room which, in th light of the torches borne by his escort, he saw had anothe occupant; then they left him, locking the heavy door be hind them; and Tarzan heard their footsteps dying awa across the courtyard as they took themselves and the torches off, leaving him in darkness.

He could not see his companion, but he could hear hi breathing. He wondered with whom fate had cast him i this remote dungeon of the city of gold.

6

The Man Who Stepped on a God

Now that the torches were gone the room was very dark, but Tarzan lost no time in starting to investigate his prison. First he groped his way to the door, which he found to be constructed of solid planking with a small, square hole cut in it about the height of his eyes. There was no sign of lock or latch upon the inside and no way of ascertaining how it was secured from the outside.

Leaving the door, Tarzan moved slowly along the walls, feeling carefully over the stone surface. He knew that the other occupant of the cell was sitting on a bench in one corner at the far end. He could still hear him breathing. As he examined the room Tarzan approached closer and closer to his fellow prisoner.

In the rear wall the ape-man discovered a window. It was small and high set. The night was so dark that he could not tell whether it opened onto the outdoors or into another apartment of the building. As an avenue of escape the window appeared quite useless, as it was much too small to accommodate the body of a man.

As Tarzan was examining the window he was close to the corner where the other man sat, and now he heard a movement there. He also noticed that the fellow's breathing had increased in rapidity, as though he were nervous or excited. At last a voice sounded through the darkness.

"What are you doing?" it demanded.

"Examining the cell," replied Tarzan.

"It will do you no good, if you are looking for a way to escape," said the voice. "You won't get out of here until they take you out, no more than I shall."

Tarzan made no reply. There seemed nothing to say; and Tarzan seldom speaks, even when others might find much to say. He went on with his examination of the room. Passing the other occupant, he felt along the fourth and last wall; but his search revealed nothing to repay the effort. He was in a small, rectangular cell of stone that was furnished with a long bench at one end and had a door and a window letting into it.

Tarzan walked to the far end of the room and sat down upon the bench. He was cold, wet, and hungry; but he was unafraid. He was thinking of all that had transpired since night had fallen and left him to the mercy of the storm; he wondered what the morrow held for him. It occurred to him that perhaps he had made a mistake in not attempting a break for liberty before his captors had succeeded in locking him in a cell from which there seemed little likelihood that he could escape at all, for in common with all animals he loathed captivity. However, here he was, locked up securely; and there seemed nothing to do but make the best of it. Some day they would take him out or unlock his cell door; then, unless he had learned that their intentions toward him were prompted by friendliness, he would take advantage of any opportunity that might be offered to escape.

Presently the man in the corner of the cell addressed him. "Who are you?" he asked. "When they brought you in I saw by the light of the torches that you are neither a Cathnean nor an Athnean." The man's voice was coarse, his tones gruff; he demanded rather than requested. This did not please Tarzan, so he did not reply. "What's the matter?" growled his fellow prisoner. "Are you dumb?" His voice was raised angrily.

"Nor deaf," replied the ape-man. "You do not have to shout at me."

The other was silent for a short time; then he spoke in an altered tone. "We may be locked in this hole together for a long time," he said. "We might as well be friends."

"As you will," replied Tarzan, his involuntary shrug passing unnoticed in the darkness of the cell.

"My name is Phobeg," said the man; "what is yours?"

"Tarzan," replied the ape-man.

"Are you either Cathnean or Athnean?"

"Neither; I am from a country far to the south."

"You would be better off had you stayed there," offered Phobeg. "How do you happen to be here in Cathne?"

"I was lost," explained the ape-man, who had no intention of telling the entire truth and thus identifying himself as a friend of one of the Cathneans' enemies. "I was caught in the flood and carried down the river to your city. Here they captured me and accused me of coming to assassinate your Queen."

"So they think you came to assassinate Nemone! Well, whether you did come for that purpose or not will make no difference."

"What do you mean?" demanded Tarzan.

"I mean that in any event you will be killed in one way or another," explained Phobeg, "whatever way will best amuse Nemone."

"Nemone is your Queen?" inquired the ape-man indifferently.

"By the mane of god, she is all that and more!" exclaimed Phobeg fervently. "Such a Queen there never has been in Onthar or Thenar before nor ever will be again. By the teeth of the great one! She makes them all stand around, the priests, the captains, and the councillors."

"But why should she have me destroyed who am only a stranger that became lost?"

"We keep no white men prisoners, only blacks as slaves. Now, were you a woman you would not be killed; and were you a very good-looking woman (not too good-looking, however) you would be assured a life of ease and luxury. But you are only a man; so you will be killed to furnish a pleasurable break in the monotony of Nemone's life."

"And what would happen to a *too* good-looking woman?" asked Tarzan.

"Enough, if Nemone saw her," replied Phobeg meaningly. "To be more beautiful than the Queen is equivalent to high treason in the estimation of Nemone. Why, men hide their wives and daughters if they think that they are too beautiful; but there are few who would risk hiding an alien prisoner.

"I know a man who has a very ugly wife," continued Phobeg, "who never comes out of her house in the daytime. She tells her neighbors that her husband keeps her hidden for fear Nemone will see her. Then there was another who *was* too beautiful. Her husband tried to keep her hidden from Nemone, but one day the Queen saw her and ordered her nose and ears cut off. Yes, I am glad that I am an ugly man rather than a beautiful woman."

"Is the Queen beautiful?" asked Tarzan.

"Yes, by the claws of the all-high, she is the most beautiful woman in the world."

"Knowing her policy, as you have explained it," remarked the ape-man, "I can readily believe that she may be the most beautiful woman in Cathne and quite sure of remaining so as long as she lives and is Queen."

"Do not mistake me," said Phobeg; "Nemone *is* beautiful; but," and he lowered his voice to a whisper, "she is a she-Satan. Even I who have served her faithfully may not look to her for mercy."

"What did you do to get here?" inquired the ape-man.

"I accidentally stepped on god's tail," replied Phobeg gloomily.

The man's strange oaths had not gone unnoticed by Tarzan, and now this latest remarkable reference to deity astounded him; but contact with strange peoples had taught him to learn certain things concerning them by observation and experience rather than by direct questioning, matters of religion being chief among these; so now he only commented, "And therefore you are being punished."

"Not yet," replied Phobeg. "The form of my punishment has not yet been decided. If Nemone has other amusements I may escape punishment, or I may come through my trial successfully and be freed; but the chances are all against me, for Nemone seldom has sufficient bloody amusement to sate her.

"Of course, if she leaves the decision of my guilt or innocence to the chances of an encounter with a single man I shall doubtless be successful in proving the latter, for I am very strong; and there is no better sword- or spear-man in Cathne; but I should have less chance against a lion, while, faced by the eternal fires of frowning Xarator, all men are guilty."

Although the man spoke the language Valthor had taught the ape-man and he understood the words, the meaning of what he said was as Greek to Tarzan. He could not quite grasp what the amusements of the Queen had to do with the administration of justice even though the inferences to be derived from Phobeg's remarks seemed apparent; the conclusion was too sinister to be entertained by the noble mind of the lord of the jungle.

He was still considering the subject and wondering about the eternal fires of frowning Xarator when sleep overcame his physical discomforts and merged his speculations with his dreams; and to the south another jungle beast crouched in the shelter of a rocky ledge while the storm that had betrayed Tarzan to new enemies wasted its waning wrath and passed on into the nothingness that is the sepulcher of storms; then as the new day dawned bright and clear he arose and stepped out into the sunlight, the great lion that we have seen before, the great lion with the golden coat and the black mane.

He sniffed the morning air and stretched, yawning. His sinuous tail twitched nervously as he looked about over the vast domain that was his because he was there, as every wilderness is the domain of the king of beasts while his majesty is in residence.

From the slight elevation upon which he stood, his yellow-green eyes surveyed a broad plain, tree dotted. There was game there in plenty: wildebeest, zebra, giraffe, koodoo, and hartebeest; and the king was hungry, for the rain had prevented his making a kill the previous night. He blinked his yellow-green eyes in the new sunlight and strode majestically down toward the plain and his breakfast, as, many miles to the north, a black slave accompanied by two warriors brought breakfast to another lord of the jungle in a prison cell at Cathne.

At the sound of footsteps approaching his prison Tarzan awoke and arose from the cold stone floor where he had been sleeping. Phobeg sat upon the edge of the wooden bench and watched the door.

"They bring us food or death," he said; "one never knows."

The ape-man made no reply. He stood there waiting until the door swung open and the slave entered with the food in a rough earthen bowl and water in a glazed jug; he looked at the two warriors standing in the open doorway and at the sunlit courtyard beyond them. What was passing in that savage mind? Perhaps the warriors would have been less at ease could they have known, but the ape-man made no move. Curiosity kept him prisoner there quite as much as armed men or sturdy door, and now he only *looked* beyond the two warriors who were eyeing him intently. They had not been on duty the night before and had not seen him, but they had heard of him. His feat with his strange weapon had been told them by their fellows.

"So this is the wild man!" exclaimed one.

"You had better be careful, Phobeg," said the other. "I should hate to be locked up in a cell with a wild man"; then, laughing at his joke, he slammed the door after the slave had come out; and the three went away.

Phobeg was appraising Tarzan with a new eye; his nakedness took on a new meaning in the light of that descriptive term, wild man. Phobeg noted the great height of his cellmate, the expanse of his chest, and his narrow hips; but he greatly underestimated the strength of the symmetrical muscles that flowed so smoothly beneath the bronzed hide; then he glanced at his own gnarled and knotted muscles and was satisfied.

"So you are a wild man!" he demanded. "How wild are you?"

Tarzan turned slowly toward the speaker. He thought that he recognized thinly veiled sarcasm in the tone of Phobeg's voice. For the first time he saw his companion in the light of day. He saw a man a few inches shorter than himself but of mighty build, a man of great girth and bulging muscles, a man who might outweigh the lord of the jungle by fifty pounds. He noted his prominent jaw, his receding forehead, and his small eyes. In silence Tarzan regarded Phobeg.

"Why don't you answer?" demanded the Cathnean.

"Do not be a fool," admonished Tarzan. "I recall that last night you said that as we might be confined here for a long time we might as well be friends. We cannot be friends by insulting one another. Food is here. Let us eat."

Phobeg grunted and inserted one of his big paws into the pot the slave had brought. As there was no knife or fork or spoon, Tarzan had no alternative but to do likewise if he wished to eat; and so he too took food from the pot with his fingers. The food was meat; it was tough and stringy and undercooked; had it been raw Tarzan had been better suited.

Phobeg chewed assiduously upon a mouthful of the meat

until he had reduced the fibers to a pulp that would pass down his throat. "An old lion must have died yesterday," he remarked, "a very old lion."

"If we acquire the characteristics of the creatures we eat, as many men believe," Tarzan replied, "we should soon die of old age on this diet."

"Yesterday I had a piece of goat's meat from Thenar," said Phobeg. "It was strong and none too tender, but it was better than this. I am accustomed to good food. In the temple the priests live as well as the nobles do in the palace, and so the temple guard lives well on the leavings of the priests. I was a member of the temple guard. I was the strongest man on the guard. I am the strongest man in Cathne. When raiders come from Thenar, or when I am taken there on raids the nobles marvel at my strength and bravery. I am afraid of nothing. With my bare hands I have killed men. Did you ever see a man like me?"

"No," admitted the ape-man.

"Yes, it is well that we should be friends," continued Phobeg, "well for you. Everyone wants to be friends with me, for they have learned that my enemies get their necks twisted. I take them like this, by the head and the neck," and with his great paws he went through a pantomime of seizing and twisting; "then, crack! their spines break. What do you think of that?"

"I should think that your enemies would find that very uncomfortable," replied Tarzan.

"Uncomfortable!" ejaculated Phobeg. "Why, man, it kills them!"

"At least they can no longer hear," commented the lord of the jungle.

"Of course they cannot hear; they are dead. I do not see what that has to do with it."

"That does not surprise me," Tarzan assured him.

"What does not surprise you?" demanded Phobeg. "That they are dead? or that they cannot hear?"

"I am not easily surprised by anything," explained the ape-man.

Beneath his low forehead Phobeg's brows were knitted in thought. He scratched his head. "What were we talking about?" he demanded.

"We were trying to decide which would be more terrible,"

explained Tarzan patiently, "to have you for a friend or an enemy."

Phobeg looked at his companion for a long time. One could almost see the laborious effort of cerebration going on beneath that thick skull. Then he shook his head. "That is not what we were talking about at all," he grumbled. "Now I have forgotten. I never saw anyone as stupid as you. When they called you a wild man they must have meant a crazy man. And I have got to remain locked in here with you for no one knows how long."

"You can always get rid of me," said Tarzan quite seriously.

"How can I get rid of you?" demanded the Cathnean.

"You can twist my neck, like this." Tarzan mimicked the pantomime in which Phobeg had explained how he rid himself of his enemies.

"I *could* do it," boasted Phobeg, "but then they *would* kill me. No, I shall let you live."

"Thanks," said Tarzan.

"Or at least while we are locked up here together," added Phobeg.

Experience had taught Tarzan that the more stupid or ignorant the man the more egotistical he was likely to be, but he had never before encountered such an example of crass stupidity and stupendous egotism as Phobeg presented. To be locked up at all with this brainless mass of flesh was bad enough in itself; but to be on bad terms with it at the same time would make matters infinitely less bearable, and so Tarzan determined to brook everything other than actual physical abuse that he might lighten the galling burden of incarceration.

Loss of liberty represented for Tarzan, as it does for all creatures endowed with brains, the acme of misery, more to be avoided than physical pain, yet, with stoic fortitude he accepted his fate without a murmur of protest; and while his body was confined between the narrow confines of four walls of stone his memories roved the jungle and the veldt and lived again the freedom and the experiences of the past.

He recalled the days of his childhood when fierce Kala, the she-ape that had suckled him at her hairy breast in his infancy, had protected him from the dangers of their savage life; and he recalled her gentleness and her patience with this backward child who must still be carried in her arms long after the balus of her companion shes were able to scurry through the trees seeking their own food and even able to protect themselves against their enemies by flight if nothing more.

These were his first impressions of life, dating back perhaps to his second year while he was still unable to swing through the trees or even make much progress upon the ground. After that he had developed rapidly, far more rapidly than a pampered child of civilization, for upon the quick development of his cunning and his strength depended his life.

With a faint smile he recalled the rage of old Tublat, his foster father, when Tarzan had deliberately undertaken to annoy him. Old "Broken-nose" had always hated Tarzan because the helplessness of his long-drawn infancy had prevented Kala from bearing other apes. Tublat had argued in the meager language of the apes that Tarzan was a weakling that would never become strong enough or clever enough to be of value to the tribe. He wanted Tarzan killed; and he tried to get old Kerchak, the king, to decree his death; so when Tarzan grew old enough to understand, he hated Tublat and sought to annoy him in every way that he could.

His memories of those days brought only smiles now, save only the great tragedy of his life, the death of Kala; but that had occurred later, when he was almost a grown man. She had been saved to him while he needed her most and not taken away until after he was amply able to fend for himself and meet the other denizens of the jungle upon an equal footing. But it was not the protection of those great arms and mighty fangs that he had missed, that he still missed even today; he had missed the maternal love of that savage heart, the only mother-love that he had ever known.

And now his thoughts turned naturally to other friends of the jungle of whom Kala had been first and greatest. There were his many friends among the great apes; there was Tantor, the elephant; there was Jad-bal-ja, the Golden Lion; there was little Nkima. Poor little Nkima! Much to his disgust and amid loud howls, Nkima had been left behind this time when Tarzan set out upon his journey into the north country; but the little monkey had contracted a cold and the ape-man did not wish to expose him to the closing rains of the rainy season.

Tarzan regretted a little that he had not brought Jad-bal-ja with him, for though he could do very well for considerable periods without the companionship of man, he often missed that of the wild beasts that were his friends. Of course the Golden Lion was sometimes an embarrassing companion when one was in contact with human beings; but he was a loyal friend and good company, for only occasionally did he break the silence.

Tarzan recalled the day that he had captured the tiny cub and how he had taught the bitch, Za, to suckle it. What a cub he had been! All lion from the very first. Tarzan sighed as he thought of the days that he and the Golden Lion had hunted and fought together.

7

Nemone

───────────────────────────────

TARZAN had thought, when he went without objection into the prison cell at Cathne, that the next morning he would be questioned and released, or at least be taken from the cell; and once out of the cell again, Tarzan had no intention of returning to it, the lord of the jungle being very certain of his own prowess.

But they had not let him out the next morning nor the next nor the next. Perhaps he might have made a break for liberty when food was brought; but each time he thought that the next day would bring his release, and waited.

Imprisonment of any nature galled him, but this experience was rendered infinitely more irksome by the presence of Phobeg. The man annoyed Tarzan; he was ignorant, a braggart, and inclined to be quarrelsome. In the interests of peace the ape-man had tolerated more from his cell-mate than he would have under ordinary circumstances; and Phobeg, being what he was, had assumed that the other's toleration was prompted by fear. Believing this, he became more arrogant and overbearing, ignorant of the fact that he was playing with death.

Phobeg had been imprisoned longer than had Tarzan, and the confinement was making him moody. Sometimes he sat for hours staring at the floor, or, at others, he would mumble to himself, carrying on long conversations which were always acrimonious and that usually resulted in working him up into a rage; then he might seek to vent his spleen upon Tarzan. The fact that Tarzan remained silent under

61

such provocation increased Phobeg's ire; but it also prevented an actual break between them, for it is still a fact, however trite the saying, that it takes two to make a quarrel; and Tarzan would not quarrel; at least, not yet.

"Nemone won't get much entertainment out of you," growled Phobeg this morning after one of his tirades had elicited no response from the ape-man.

"Well, even so," replied Tarzan, "you should more than make up to her any amusement value that I may lack."

"That I will," exclaimed Phobeg. "If it is fighting she wants, she shall see such fighting as she has never seen before when she matches Phobeg with either man or beast; but you! Bah! She will have to pit you against some half-grown child if she wishes to see any fight at all. You have no courage; your veins are filled with water. If she is wise she will dump you into Xarator. By god's tail! I should like to see you there. I'll bet my best habergeon they could hear you scream in Athne."

The ape-man was standing gazing at the little rectangle of sky that he could see through the small, barred opening in the door. He remained silent after Phobeg had ceased speaking, totally ignoring him as though he had not spoken, as though he did not exist. Phobeg became furious. He rose from the bench upon which he had been sitting.

"Coward!" he cried. "Why don't you answer me? By the yellow fangs of Thoos! I've a mind to beat some manners into you, so that you will know enough to answer when your betters speak." He took a step in the direction of the ape-man.

Slowly Tarzan turned toward the angry man, his level gaze fixed upon the other's eyes, and waited. He said nothing, but his attitude was an open book that even the stupid Phobeg could read. And Phobeg hesitated.

Just what might have happened no man may know, for at that instant four warriors came and swung the door of the cell open. "Come with us," said one of them, "both of you."

Phobeg sullenly, Tarzan with the savage dignity of Numa, accompanied the four warriors across the open courtyard and through a doorway that led into a long corridor at the end of which they were ushered into a large room. Here, behind a table, sat seven warriors trapped in ivory and gold. Among them Tarzan recognized the two who had questioned

him the night of his capture, old Tomos and the younger
Gemnon.

"These are nobles," whispered Phobeg to Tarzan. "That
one at the center of the table is old Tomos, the Queen's
councillor. He would like to marry the Queen, but I guess he
is too old to suit her. The one on his right is Erot. He used
to be a common warrior like me; but Nemone took a fancy
to him, and now he is the Queen's favorite. She won't marry
him though, for he is not of noble blood. The young fellow
on Tomos' left is Gemnon. He is from an old and noble
family. Warriors who have served him say he is a very decent sort."

As Phobeg gossiped, the two prisoners and their guard
had been standing just inside the doorway waiting to be
summoned to advance, and Tarzan had had an opportunity
to note the architecture and furnishings of the room. The
ceiling was low and was supported by a series of engaged
columns at regular intervals about the four walls. Between
the columns along one side of the room behind the table at
which the nobles were seated were unglazed windows, and
there were three doorways: that through which Tarzan and
Phobeg had been brought, which was directly opposite the
windows, and one at either end of the room. The doors
themselves were beautifully carved and highly polished,
some of the panels containing mosaics of gold and ivory
and bits of colored substances.

The floor was of stone, composed of many pieces of different shapes and sizes; but all so nicely fitted that joints
were barely discernible. On the floor were a few small rugs
either of the skins of lions or of a stiff and heavy wool
weave. These latter contained simple designs in several col-
ors and resembled the work of primitive people such as the
Navajos of southwestern America.

Upon the walls were paintings depicting battle scenes in
which lions and elephants took part with warriors, and always the warriors with the elephants appeared to be suffering defeat, while the warriors with the lions were collect-
ing many heads from fallen foemen. Above these mural
paintings was a row of mounted heads encircling the room.
These were similar to those Tarzan had seen in the guardroom the night of his coming to Cathne and differed from
them only in that they were better specimens and better

mounted. Perhaps, too, the heads of men predominated here, scowling down upon their enemies.

But now Tarzan's examination of the room was interrupted by the voice of Tomos. "Bring the prisoners forward," he directed the under-officer who was one of the four warriors escorting them.

When the two men had been halted upon the opposite side of the table from the nobles, Tomos pointed at Tarzan's companion. "Which is this one?" he demanded.

"He is called Phobeg," replied the under-officer.

"What is the charge against him?"

"He profaned Thoos."

"Who brought the charge?"

"The high priest."

"It was an accident," Phobeg hastened to explain. "I meant no disrespect."

"Silence!" snapped Tomos. Then he pointed at Tarzan. "And this one?" he demanded. "Who is he?"

"This is the one who calls himself Tarzan," explained Gemnon. "You will recall that you and I examined him the night he was captured."

"Yes, yes," said Tomos; "I recall. He carried some sort of strange weapon."

"Is he the man of whom you told me," asked Erot, "the one who came from Athne to assassinate the Queen?"

"This is the one," replied Tomos; "he came at night during the last storm and succeeded in making his way into the palace grounds after dark before he was discovered and arrested."

"He does not greatly resemble an Athnean," commented Erot.

"I am not," said Tarzan.

"Silence!" commanded Tomos.

"Why should I be silent?" demanded Tarzan. "There is none other to speak for me than myself; therefore I shall speak for myself. I am no enemy of your people, nor are my people at war with yours. I demand my liberty!"

"He demands his liberty," mimicked Erot and laughed aloud as though it was a good joke; "the slave *demands* his liberty!"

Tomos half rose from his seat, his face purple with rage. He banged the table with his fist. He pointed a finger at

Tarzan. "Speak when you are spoken to, slave, and not otherwise; and when Tomos, the councillor, tells you to be silent, be silent."

"I have spoken," said Tarzan; "when I choose to speak again, I shall speak."

"We have a way of silencing impudent slaves, forever," sneered Erot.

"It is evident that he is a man from a far country," interjected Gemnon. "It is not strange that he neither understands our customs nor recognizes the great among us. Perhaps we should listen to him. If he is not an Athnean and no enemy, why should we imprison him or punish him?"

"He came over the palace walls at night," retorted Tomos. "He could have come for but one purpose, to kill our Queen; therefore he must die. The manner of his death shall be at the pleasure of Nemone, our sweet and gracious Queen."

"He told us that the river washed him down to Cathne," persisted Gemnon. "It was a very dark night and he did not know where he was when he finally succeeded in crawling ashore; it was only chance that brought him to the palace."

"A pretty story but not plausible," countered Erot.

"Why not plausible?" demanded Gemnon. "I think it quite plausible. We know that no man could have swum the river in the flood that was raging that night, and that this man could not have reached the spot at which he climbed the wall except by swimming the river or crossing the bridge of gold. We know that he did not cross the bridge, because the bridge was well guarded and no one crossed that night. Knowing therefore that he did not cross the bridge and could not have swum the river, we know that the only way he could have reached that particular spot upon the river's bank was by being swept downstream from above. I believe his story, and I believe that we should treat him as an honorable warrior from some distant kingdom until we have better reasons than we now have for believing otherwise."

"I should not care to be the one to defend a man who came here to kill the Queen," sneered Erot meaningly.

"Enough of this!" said Tomos curtly. "The man shall be judged fairly and destroyed as Nemone thinks best."

As he ceased speaking, a door at one end of the room opened and a noble resplendent in ivory and gold stepped into the chamber. Halting just within the threshold, he faced the nobles at the table.

"The Queen!" he announced in a loud voice and then stepped aside.

All eyes turned in the direction of the doorway and at the same time the nobles rose to their feet and then kneeled upon the floor, facing the doorway through which the Queen would enter. The warriors on guard, including those with Tarzan and Phobeg, did likewise, Phobeg following their example. Everyone in the room kneeled except the noble who had announced the Queen, or rather every Cathnean. Tarzan of the Apes did not kneel.

"Down, jackal!" growled one of the guards in a whisper, and then amidst deathly silence a woman stepped into view and paused, framed in the carved casing of the doorway. Regal, she stood there glancing indolently about the apartment; then her eyes met those of the ape-man and, for a moment, held there on his. A slight frown of puzzlement contracted her straight brows as she continued on into the room, approaching the table and the kneeling men.

Behind her followed a half dozen richly arrayed nobles, resplendent in burnished gold and gleaming ivory, but as they crossed the chamber Tarzan saw only the gorgeous figure of the Queen. She was clothed more simply than her escort; but that form, which her apparel revealed rather than hid, required no embellishments other than those with which nature had endowed it. She was far more beautiful than the crude Phobeg had painted her.

A narrow diadem set with red stones encircled her brow, confining her glossy black hair; upon either side of her head, covering her ears, a large golden disc depended from the diadem; while from its rear rose a slender filament of gold that curved forward, supporting a large red stone above the center of her head. About her throat was a simple golden band that held a brooch and pendant of ivory in the soft hollow of her neck. Upon her upper arms were similar golden bands supporting triangular, curved ornaments of ivory. A broad band of gold mesh supported her breasts, the band being embellished with horizontal bands of red stones, while from its upper edge depended five narrow triangles of ivory, a large one in the center and two smaller ones on either side.

A girdle about her hips was of gold mesh. It supported another ivory triangle the slender apex of which curved slightly inward between her legs and also her scant skirt of black monkey hair that fell barely to her knees, conforming perfectly to the contours of her body.

About her wrists were numerous bracelets of ivory and gold and around her ankles were vertical strips of ivory held together by leather thongs, identical in form to those worn by Valthor and by the Cathnean men. Her feet were shod with dainty sandals; and as she moved upon them silently across the stone floor, her movements seemed to Tarzan a combination of the seductive languor of the sensualist and the sinuous grace and savage alertness of the tigress.

That she was marvellously beautiful by the standards of any land or any time grew more apparent to the lord of the jungle as she came nearer to him, yet her presence exhaled a subtle essence that left him wondering if her beauty were the reflection of a nature all good or all evil, for her mien and bearing suggested that there could be no compromise— Nemone, the Queen, was all one or all the other.

She kept her eyes upon him as she crossed the room slowly, and Tarzan did not drop his own from hers. There was neither boldness nor rudeness in his gaze, perhaps there was not even interest—it was the noncommittal, cautious appraisal of the wild beast that watches a creature which it neither fears nor desires.

The quizzical frown still furrowed Nemone's smooth brow as she reached the end of the table where the nobles kneeled. It was not an angry frown, and there might have been in it much of interest and something of amusement, for unusual things interested and amused Nemone, so rare were they in the monotony of her life; and it was certainly unusual to see one who did not accord her the homage due a queen.

As she halted she turned her eyes upon the kneeling nobles. "Arise!" she commanded, and in that single word the vibrant qualities of her rich, deep voice sent a strange thrill through the ape-man. "Who is this that does not kneel to Nemone?" she demanded, her gaze now returned to the bronzed figure standing impassively before her.

As Tarzan had been standing behind the nobles as they had turned to face Nemone when they kneeled, only two of his guards had been aware of his dereliction; but now as they arose and faced about, their countenances were filled with horror and rage when they discovered that the strange captive had so affronted their Queen.

Tomos went purple again. He spluttered with rage. "He is an ignorant and impudent savage, my Queen," he said; "but as he is about to die his actions are of no consequence."

"Why is he about to die?" demanded Nemone, "and how is he to die?"

"He is to die because he came here in the dead of night to assassinate your majesty," explained Tomos; "the manner of his death rests of course in the hands of our gracious Queen."

Nemone's dark eyes, veiled behind long lashes, appraised the ape-man, lingering upon his bronzed skin and the rolling contours of his muscles; then rising to the handsome face until her eyes met his. "Why did you not kneel?" she asked.

"Why should I kneel to you who they have said will have me killed?" demanded Tarzan. "Why should I kneel to you who are not my Queen? Why should I, Tarzan of the Apes, who kneels to no one, kneel to you?"

"Silence!" cried Tomos. "Your impertinence knows no bounds. Do you not realize, ignorant slave, low savage, that you are addressing Nemone, the Queen!"

Tarzan made no reply; he did not even look at Tomos; his eyes were fixed upon Nemone. She fascinated him; but whether as a thing of beauty or a thing of evil, he did not know. He only knew that few women, other than La, the High Priestess of the Flaming God, had ever so wholly aroused his interest and his curiosity.

Tomos turned to the under-officer in command of the escort that was guarding Tarzan and Phobeg. "Take them away!" he snapped. "Take them back to their cell until we are ready to destroy them."

"Wait," said Nemone. "I would know more of this man," and then she turned to Tarzan. "So you came to kill me!" Her voice was smooth, almost caressing. At the moment the woman reminded Tarzan of a cat that is playing with its victim. "Perhaps they chose a good man for the purpose; you look as though you might be equal to any feat of arms."

"Killing a woman is no feat of arms," replied Tarzan. "I do not kill women. I did not come here to kill you."

"Then why did you come to Onthar?" inquired the Queen in her silky voice.

"That I have already explained twice to that old man with the red face," replied Tarzan, nodding in the general direction of Tomos. "Ask him; I am tired of explaining to people who have already decided to kill me."

Tomos trembled with rage and half drew his slender, dagger-like sword. "Let me destroy him, my Queen," he cried. "Let me wipe out the affront he has put upon my beloved ruler."

Nemone had flushed angrily at Tarzan's words, but she did not lose control of herself. "Sheathe your sword, Tomos," she commanded icily; "Nemone is competent to decide when she is affronted and what steps to take. The fellow is indeed impertinent; but it seems to me that if he affronted anyone, it was Tomos he affronted and not Nemone. However, his temerity shall not go unpunished. Who is this other?"

"He is a temple guard named Phobeg," explained Erot. "He profaned Thoos."

"It would amuse us," said Nemone, "to see these two men fight upon the Field of the Lions. Let them fight without other weapons than those which Thoos has given them. To the victor, freedom," she hesitated momentarily, "freedom within limits. Take them away!"

8

Upon the Field of the Lions

ARZAN and Phobeg were back in their little stone cell;
the ape-man had not escaped. He had had no opportunity to escape on the way back to his prison, for
the warriors who guarded him had redoubled their vigilance,
having been cautioned to do so by Erot, and the points of two
spears had been kept constantly against his body.

Phobeg was moody and thoughtful. The attitude of his
fellow prisoner during their examination by the nobles, his
seeming indifference to the majesty and power of Nemone,
had tended to alter Phobeg's former estimate of the ape-man's
courage. He realized now that the fellow was either a
very brave man or a very great fool; and he hoped that he
was the latter, for Phobeg was to be pitted against him
upon the Field of the Lions, possibly on the morrow.

Phobeg was stupid, but past experience had taught him
something of the psychology of mortal combat. He knew
that when a man went into battle fearing his antagonist he
was already handicapped and partly defeated. Now Phobeg
did not fear Tarzan; he was too stupid and too ignorant to
anticipate fear. Facing probable defeat and death, he could
be overcome by fear and even cowardice; but he was of
too low an order, mentally, to visualize either in imagination, except in a rather vague and hazy way.

Tarzan, on the other hand, was of an entirely different
temperament; and though he never knew fear it was for a
very different reason. Being intelligent and imaginative, he
could visualize all the possibilities of an impending encoun-

70

ter; but he could never know fear, because death held no
terrors for him; and he had learned to suffer physical pain
without the usually attendant horrors of mental anguish.
Therefore, if he thought about the coming combat at all, he
was not overconfident nor fearful nor nervous. Could he
have known what was in the fellow's mind when he commenced to speak he would have been amused.

"It will doubtless be tomorrow," said Phobeg grimly.

"What will be tomorrow?" inquired the ape-man.

"The combat in which I shall kill you," explained the
cheerful Phobeg.

"Oh, so you are going to kill me! Phobeg, I am surprised.
I thought that you were my friend." Tarzan's tone was serious, though a brighter man than Phobeg might have discovered in it a note of banter; but Phobeg was not bright at
all, and he thought that Tarzan was already commencing
to throw himself upon his mercy.

"It will soon be over," Phobeg assured him. "I promise
that I shall not let you suffer long."

"I suppose that you will twist my neck like this," said
Tarzan, pretending to twist something with his two hands.

"M-m-m, perhaps," admitted Phobeg; "but I shall have
to throw you about a bit first. We must amuse Nemone, you
know."

"Surely, by all means!" assented Tarzan. "But suppose
you should not be able to throw me about? Suppose that I
should throw you about? Would that amuse Nemone? Or
perhaps it would amuse you!"

Phobeg laughed. "It amuses me very much just to think
about it," he said, "and I hope that it amuses you to think
about it, for that is as near as you will ever come to throwing Phobeg about; have I not told you that I am the strongest man in Cathne?"

"Oh, of course," admitted Tarzan. "I had forgotten that
for the moment."

"You would do well to try to remember it," advised Phobeg, "or otherwise our combat will not be interesting at all."

"And Nemone would not be amused! That would be sad.
We should make it as interesting and exciting as possible,
and you must not conclude it too soon."

"You are right about that," agreed Phobeg. "The better it
is the more generous will Nemone feel toward me when it

is over; she may even give me a donation in addition to my liberty if we amuse her well.

"By the belly of Thoos!" he exclaimed, slapping his thigh. "We must make a good fight of it and a long one. Now listen! How would this be? At first we shall pretend that you are defeating me; I shall let you throw me about a bit. You see? Then I shall get the better of it for a while, and then you. We shall take turns up to a certain point, and then, when I give you the cue, you must pretend to be frightened, and run away from me. I shall then chase you all over the arena, and that will give them a good laugh. When I catch you at last (and you must let me catch you right in front of Nemone) I shall then twist your neck and kill you, but I will do it as painlessly as possible."

"You are very kind," said Tarzan grimly.

"Do you like the plan?" demanded Phobeg. "Is it not a splendid one?"

"It will certainly amuse them," agreed Tarzan, "if it works."

"If it works! Why should it not work? It will, if you do your part."

"But suppose *I* kill *you?*" inquired the lord of the jungle.

"There you go again!" exclaimed Phobeg. "I must say that you are a good fellow after all, for you will have your little joke; and I can tell you that there is no one who enjoys a little joke more than Phobeg."

"I hope that you are in the same mood tomorrow," remarked Tarzan.

When the next day dawned the slave and the guard came with a large breakfast for the two prisoners, the best meal that had been served them since they had been imprisoned.

"Eat well," advised one of the warriors, "that you may have strength to fight a good fight for the entertainment of the Queen. For one of you it is the last meal; so you had both better enjoy it to the full, since there is no telling for which one of you it is the last."

"It is the last for him," said Phobeg, jerking a thumb in the direction of Tarzan.

"It is thus that the betting goes," said the warrior, "but even so one cannot always be sure. The stranger is a large man, and he looks strong."

"There is none so strong as Phobeg," the former temple guard reminded them.

The warrior shrugged. "Perhaps," he admitted, "but I am not betting any money on either of you."

"Twenty drachmas to ten that he runs away from me before the fight is over," offered Phobeg.

"And if he kills you, who will pay me?" demanded the warrior. "No, that is not a good bet," and he went out and closed and locked the door behind him.

An hour later a large detachment of warriors came and took Tarzan and Phobeg from the prison. They led them through the palace grounds and out into an avenue bordered by old trees. It was a lovely avenue flanked by the white and gold homes of the nobles and the great two-storied palace surmounted by its golden domes.

Here were throngs of people waiting to see the start of the pageant and companies of warriors standing at ease, leaning upon their spears. It was an interesting sight to Tarzan who had been so long confined in the gloomy prison. He noted the dress of the civilians and the architecture of the splendid houses that could be glimpsed between the trees. He saw that the men wore short tunics or jerkins that were quite similar to the habergeons worn by the warriors, except that they were of a solid piece of cloth or light leather rather than of discs of elephant hide. The women wore short skirts of hair or cloth or leather, scant, clinging skirts that terminated just above the knees; a band to confine the breasts, sandals, and ornaments completed their simple attire.

Tarzan and Phobeg were escorted west along the avenue; and as they passed, the crowd commented upon them. There were many who knew Phobeg; some shouted encouragement to him; others taunted and insulted him. It appeared that Phobeg's popularity was not city wide. They discussed Tarzan freely but with no malice. He interested them, and there was much speculation as to his chances in a fight against the burly temple guard. The ape-man heard many wagers offered and taken; some were on him and some against; but it was evident that Phobeg was the favored of the bettors.

At the end of the avenue Tarzan saw the great bridge of gold that spanned the river. It was a splendid structure

built entirely of the precious metal. Two golden lions of
heroic size flanked the approach from the city, and as he
was led across the bridge the ape-man saw two identical
lions guarding the western end.

Out upon the plain that is called the Field of the Lions
a crowd of spectators was filing toward a point about a
mile from the city where many people were congregated,
and toward this assemblage the detachment escorted the
two gladiators. Here was a large, oval arena excavated
to a depth of twenty or thirty feet in the floor of the
plain. Upon the excavated earth piled symmetrically around
the edges of the pit, and terraced from the plain level to
the top, were arranged slabs of stone to serve as seats.
At the east end of the arena was a wide ramp descending
into it. Spanning the ramp was a low arch surmounted by
the loges of the Queen and high nobility.

As Tarzan passed beneath the arch and descended the
ramp toward the arena, he saw that nearly half the seats
were already taken. The people were eating food that they
had brought with them, and there was much laughter and
talking. Evidently it was a gala day. He asked Phobeg.

"This is part of the celebration that annually follows the
ending of the rainy season," explained the Cathnean. "There
is entertainment of some sort here at least once a month
and oftener when the weather permits. You will have an
opportunity to see all the events before I kill you, as our
combat will undoubtedly be the last event upon the pro-
gram."

The warriors conducted the two men to the far end of
the arena where a terrace had been cut part way up the
sloping side of the arena, a wooden ladder leaning against
the wall giving access to it. Here, upon this terrace, Tarzan
and Phobeg were installed with a few warriors to serve
as guards.

Presently, from the direction of the city, Tarzan heard
the music of drums and trumpets.

"Here they come!" cried Phobeg.

"Who?" asked Tarzan.

"The Queen and the lion men," replied his adversary.

"What are the lion men?" inquired Tarzan.

"They are the nobles," explained Phobeg. "Really only
the hereditary nobles are members of the clan of lions,

but we usually speak of all nobles as lion men. Erot is a noble because Nemone has created him one; but he is not a lion man, as he was not born a noble."

"Cleave my skull! but I bet he hates that," commented one of the guard.

"He'd give a right eye to be a lion man," said Phobeg.

"It's too late now," observed the warrior; "he should have picked his parents more carefully."

"He claims that he did pick a noble father," explained Phobeg, "but his mother denies it."

Another warrior laughed. "Son of a noble!" he scoffed. "I know old Tibdos, the husband of Erot's mother; I know him well. He cleans the lions' cages at the breeding farm. Erot looks just like him. Son of a noble!"

"Son of a she-jackal!" growled Phobeg. "I wish I were to fight him today instead of this poor fellow."

"You feel sorry for him?" inquired a warrior.

"Yes, in a way," replied Phobeg. "He is not a half·bad fellow, and I have nothing against him except that he is stupid. He cannot seem to understand the simplest things. He does not seem to realize that I am the strongest man in Cathne and that I am going to kill him this afternoon, unless they get through with the other events early and I kill him this morning."

"How do you know that he does not realize these things?" demanded the warrior.

"Because he has never given any sign that he is very much afraid."

"Possibly he does not believe that you can kill him," suggested the warrior.

"Than that proves that he is very stupid; but stupid or not, I am going to kill him. I am going to twist his neck until his spine breaks. I can scarcely wait to get my hands on him; of all the things that I love there is no sensation equal to that of killing a man. I love that better than I love women."

Tarzan glanced at the great hulk squatting beside him. "The French have a word for that," he remarked.

"I do not know what you are talking about," growled Phobeg.

"I am not surprised."

"There he goes again!" exclaimed Phobeg. "What sense

is there to that? Did I not tell you that he is stupid?"

Now the blaring of the trumpets and the beating of the drums burst with increased volume upon their ears, and Tarzan saw that the musicians were marching down the ramp into the arena at the far end of the great oval. At the same time the tumult in the stands increased as new thousands surged over the rim of the stadium and sought seats among the thousands already there.

Behind the music marched a company of warriors, and from each spear head fluttered a colored pennon. It was a stirring and colorful picture, but nothing to what followed.

A few yards in rear of the warriors came a chariot of gold drawn by four maned lions, where, half reclining upon a couch draped with furs and gaily colored cloths, rode Nemone, the Queen. Sixteen black slaves held the lions in leash; and at either side of the chariot marched six nobles resplendent in gold and ivory, while a huge black, marching behind, held a great, red parasol over the Queen. Squatting upon little seats above the rear wheels of the chariot were two small blackamoors wielding feathered fans above her.

At sight of the chariot and its royal occupant, the people in the stands arose and then kneeled down in salute to their ruler, while wave after wave of applause rolled round the amphitheater as the pageant slowly circled the arena.

Behind Nemone's chariot marched another company of warriors; these were followed by a number of gorgeously decorated wooden chariots, each drawn by two lions and driven by a noble; following these marched a company of nobles on foot, while a third company of warriors brought up the rear.

When the column had circled the arena Nemone quit her chariot and ascended to her loge above the ramp amid the continued cheering of the populace, the chariots driven by the nobles lined up in the center of the arena, the royal guard formed across the entrance to the stadium, and the nobles who had no part in the games went to their private loges.

There followed then in quick succession contests in dagger throwing and in the throwing of spears, feats of strength and skill, and foot races. Upon every event wagers were laid and the whole stadium was a bedlam of shouted wagers and odds, of curses, groans, hoots, laughter, and applause.

In the loges of Nemone and the nobles great sums changed hands upon every event. The Queen was an inveterate gambler, winning or losing a fortune upon the cast of a single dagger. When she won she smiled, and she smiled too when she lost; but men knew that contestants upon whom Nemone won regularly through the year were the recipients of royal favors, while those upon whom she consistently lost often disappeared.

When the minor sports were completed the chariot races began; and upon these the betting dwarfed all the other betting of the day, and men and women acted like maniacs as they encouraged a favorite driver, applauded a winner, or berated an unfortunate loser.

Two drivers raced in each event, the distance being always the same, one lap of the arena, for lions cannot maintain high speed for great distances. After each race the winner received a pennon from the Queen, while the loser drove up the ramp and out of the stadium amid the hoots of those who had lost money on him. Then two more raced, and when the last pair had finished the winners paired off for new events. Thus, by elimination, the contestants were eventually reduced to two, winners in each event in which they had contested. This, then, was the première racing event of the day, and the noise and the betting that it engendered surpassed all that had gone before.

The winner of this final race was acclaimed champion of the day and was presented with a golden helmet by Nemone herself, and even those who had bet upon his rival and lost their money added their voices to the ovation that the noisy throng accorded him as he drove proudly around the arena and disappeared up the ramp beneath the arch of the Queen, his golden helmet shining bravely in the sun.

"Now," said Phobeg in a loud voice, "the people are going to see something worth while. It is what they have been waiting for, and they will not be disappointed. If you have a god, fellow, pray to him, for you are about to die."

"Are you not going to permit me to run around the arena first while you chase me?" demanded Tarzan.

9

"Death! Death!"

A SCORE of slaves were busily cleaning up the arena following the departure of the lion-drawn chariots, the audience was standing and stretching itself, nobles were wandering from loge to loge visiting their friends, men and women were settling up past wagers and making new ones. The sounds of many voices enveloped the stadium in one mighty discord. The period was one of intermission between events.

Tarzan was annoyed. Crowds irritated his nerves. The sound of human voices was obnoxious to him. Through narrowed lids he surveyed the scene. If ever a wild beast looked upon its enemies it was then.

Phobeg was still boasting in a loud voice that was clearly audible to at least a portion of the audience sitting just above the gladiators' ledge. The attitude of the temple guard was anything but soothing to the lord of the jungle, but by no sign did he intimate that he heard him after his first retort.

Already the betting was running high on this last event of the day, though only a small proportion of the audience had had a fair view of the two contestants by which they might compare them. Phobeg, however, was known by reputation and was the favorite, the odds running as high as ten to one against Tarzan.

In the royal loge Nemone lay back luxuriously in the great chair that was half a throne and half a couch. She had lost heavily during the day, but she showed no ill humor. However, the nobles surrounding her were ill at ease and hoped that she would win on this last event. Each was determined to bet heavily upon the strange wild man with Nemone, so that she might win back all that she had lost to them upon earlier events, for all were assured that Nemone would back Phobeg, it being her custom to bet heavily upon all favorites.

Erot was particularly anxious that the Queen should win back what he had won from her. For some time he had been a trifle uncertain as to his position in the good graces of his sovereign; he had sensed, perhaps, that he was slipping a little; and he had had sufficient experience to know that winning money from Nemone constituted nothing less than a tremendous shove to one who had started to slip.

Therefore Erot, with the other nobles, having determined to let Nemone win their money on Phobeg sent slaves out into the audience secretly to place money enough on Phobeg to reimburse them what they lost to Nemone on Tarzan. The plan was accurately figured and neatly worked, and when the day was over Nemone would be winner and so would they, all of their losses having been more than made up by their winnings on Phobeg, which the common people would have paid.

This large volume of money going suddenly among the audience which was already favoring Phobeg and offering large odds against Tarzan found very little Tarzan money available at ten to one. The natural result was that to place their money at all they had to offer larger odds, and to reimburse themselves of their losses to Nemone, or rather their assumed losses, for no wagers had yet been laid in the royal loge, they were compelled to put up enormous sums as the odds soared upward finally until it took one hundred Phobeg drachmas to cover one of Tarzan's.

Now a trumpet sounded, and the warriors guarding Tarzan and Phobeg ordered them down into the arena and paraded them once around it that the people might compare the gladiators and choose a favorite. As they passed before the royal loge Nemone leaned forward with half-closed eyes surveying the tall stranger and the squat Cathnean.

Erot, the Queen's favorite, watched her. "A thousand drachmas on the stranger!" he cried.

"I am betting on the stranger, too," interjected another noble eagerly.

"So am I," said Nemone.

Erot and the other nobles were amazed; this upset their plans completely. Of course they would win more money, but one always felt safer losing to Nemone than winning from her.

"You will lose your money," Erot told her.

"Then why did you offer to bet on the stranger?" demanded the Queen.

"The odds were so attractive that I was tempted into taking a chance," explained Erot quickly.

"What are the odds now?"

"One hundred to one."

"And you think the stranger may not have even one chance in a hundred of winning?" demanded Nemone, toying idly with the hilt of her dagger.

"Phobeg is the strongest man in Cathne," said Erot. "I really think that the stranger has no chance at all against him; he is as good as dead already."

"Very well then, if you feel that way about it you should bet on Phobeg," whispered Nemone softly. "I am going to wager 100,000 drachmas on the stranger. How much of this do you wish, my dear Erot?"

"I wish that my Queen would not risk her money on him at all," said Erot; "I am grieved when my beloved Queen loses."

"You bore me, Erot." Nemone gestured impatiently and then, turning to the other nobles, "Is there none here who will cover my drachmas?"

Instantly they were all eager to accomodate her. To win a hundred thousand drachmas from the Queen in addition to all that they would win from the common people was too much for their cupidity; they even forgot Nemone's possible wrath in their anxiety to accommodate her now that it was certain that her decision could not be altered, and in a few minutes the bets had been recorded.

"He has a fine physique," commented Nemone, her eyes upon the jungle lord, "and he is taller than the other."

"But look at Phobeg's muscles," Erot reminded her. "This Phobeg has killed many men; they say that he twists their necks and breaks their spines."

"We shall see," was the Queen's only comment.

Erot thought that he would not like to be in Phobeg's sandals, for if the stranger did not kill him Nemone most certainly would see that he did not long survive, who had robbed her of a hundred thousand drachmas.

Now the two men were posted in the arena a short distance from the royal loge, and the captain of the stadium was giving them their instructions which were extremely simple: they were to remain inside the arena and try to kill one another with their bare hands, though the use of elbows, knees, feet, or teeth was not barred; there were no other rules governing the combat. The winner was to receive his freedom, though even this had been qualified by Nemone.

"When the trumpet sounds you may attack," said the captain of the stadium. "And may Thoos be with you."

Tarzan and Phobeg had been placed ten paces apart. Now they stood waiting the signal. Phobeg swelled his chest and beat upon it with his fists; he flexed his arms, swelling the great muscles of his biceps until they stood out like great knotty balls; then he hopped about, warming up his leg muscles. He was attracting all the attention, and that pleased him excessively.

Tarzan stood quietly, his arms folded loosely across his chest, his muscles relaxed. He appeared totally unconscious of the presence of the noisy multitude or even of Phobeg, but he was not unconscious of anything that was transpiring about him. His eyes and his ears were alert; it would be Tarzan who would hear the first note of the trumpet's signal; Tarzan was ready!

Tarzan cared nothing for the stupid men-things making silly noises in their throats, gathered here to see two fellow creatures that had never harmed them try to kill one another for their pleasure; he did not care what they thought about him; to him they were less than the droppings of lions that the slaves had swept up in the arena.

He did not wish to kill Phobeg, nor did he wish to be killed; but Phobeg disgusted him, and he would have liked to punish the man for his ridiculous egotism. He realized that his antagonist was a mighty man and that it might not be an easy thing to punish him without taking a great deal of punishment himself, but this risk he did not mind so that he could halt his own punishment short of crippling or death. His gaze chanced to cross the royal loge; it halted there; the eyes of Nemone met his and held them. What strange eyes were hers—so beautiful, with fires burning far beneath the surface, so mysterious!

The trumpet pealed, and Tarzan's eyes swung back to Phobeg. A strange silence fell upon the amphitheater. The two men approached one another, Phobeg strutting and confident, Tarzan with the easy, graceful stride of a lion.

"Say your prayers, fellow!" shouted the temple guard. "I am going to kill you; but first I shall play with you for the amusement of Nemone."

Phobeg came closer and reached for Tarzan. The ape-man let him seize him by the shoulders; then Tarzan cupped his two hands and brought the heels of them up suddenly and with great force beneath Phobeg's chin and at the same time pushed the man from him. The great head snapped back, and the fellow's huge bulk hurtled backward a dozen paces, where Phobeg sat down heavily.

A groan of surprise arose from the audience, interspersed with cheers from those who had wagered on Tarzan. Phobeg scrambled to his feet; his face was contorted with rage; in an instant he had gone berserk. With a roar, he charged the ape-man.

"No quarter!" he screamed. "I kill you *now!*"

"Kill! Kill!" shouted the Phobeg adherents. "Death! Death! Give us a death!"

"Don't you wish to throw me about a bit first?" asked Tarzan in a low voice, as he lightly side-stepped the other's mad charge.

"No!" screamed Phobeg, turning clumsily and charging again. "I kill! I kill!"

Tarzan caught the outstretched hands and spread them wide; then a bronzed arm, lightninglike, clamped about Phobeg's short neck; the ape-man wheeled suddenly about, leaned forward, and hurled his antagonist over his head. Phobeg fell heavily to the sandy gravel of the arena.

Nemone leaned from the royal loge, her eyes flashing, her bosom heaving. Erot was but one of many nobles who experienced a constriction of the diaphragm. Nemone turned to him. "Would you like to bet a little more on the strongest man in Cathne?" she asked.

Erot smiled a sickly smile. "The battle has only commenced," he said.

"But already it is as good as over," taunted Nemone.

Phobeg arose but this time more slowly, nor did he charge again but approached his antagonist warily; his tactics now were very different from what they had been. He wanted to get close enough to Tarzan to get a hold; that was all he desired, just a hold; then, he knew, he could crush the man with his great strength.

Perhaps the ape-man sensed what was in the mind of his foe, perhaps it was just chance that caused him to taunt Phobeg by holding his left wrist out to the other; but whatever it was, Phobeg seized upon the opportunity and, grasping Tarzan's wrist, sought to drag the ape-man into his embrace; then Tarzan stepped in quickly, struck Phobeg a terrific blow in the face with his right fist, seized the wrist of the hand that held his, and, again whirling quickly beneath his victim, threw him heavily once more, using Phobeg's arm as a lever and his own shoulder as a fulcrum.

This time Phobeg had difficulty in arising at all. He came up very slowly. The ape-man was standing over him. The blood froze in the veins of the Cathnean as he heard the low, beastlike growl rumbling in the throat of the stranger.

Suddenly Tarzan stooped and seized Phobeg, and, lifting him bodily, held him above his head. "Shall I run now, Phobeg?" he growled, "or are you too tired to chase me?" Then he hurled the man to the ground again a little nearer to the royal loge where Nemone sat, tense and thrilling.

Like a lion with its prey, the lord of the jungle followed the man who had taunted him and would have killed him; twice again he picked him up and hurled him closer to the end of the arena. Now the fickle crowd was screaming to Tarzan to kill Phobeg; Phobeg, the strongest man in Cathne; Phobeg, who twisted men's necks until their spines cracked.

Again Tarzan seized his antagonist and held him above his head. Phobeg struggled weakly, but he was quite helpless. Tarzan walked to the side of the arena near the royal loge and hurled the great body up into the audience.

"Take your strong man," he said; "Tarzan does not want

him." Then he walked away and stood before the ramp, waiting, as though he demanded his freedom.

Amid shrieks and howls that called to Tarzan's mind only the foulest of wild beasts, the loathsome hyena, the crowd hurled the unhappy Phobeg back into the arena. "Kill him! Kill him!" they screamed.

Nemone leaned from her loge. "Kill him, Tarzan!" she cried.

Tarzan shrugged with disgust and turned away.

"Kill him, slave!" commanded a noble from his luxurious loge.

"I shall not kill him," replied the ape-man.

Nemone arose in her loge. She was flushed and excited. "Tarzan!" she cried, and when the ape-man glanced up at her, "why do you not kill him?"

"Why should I kill him?" demanded Tarzan. "He cannot harm me, and I kill only in self-defense or for food; but I do not eat human flesh, so why should I kill him?"

Phobeg, bruised, battered, and helpless, arose weakly to his feet and stood reeling drunkenly. He heard the voice of the pitiless mob screaming for his death. He saw his antagonist standing a few paces away in front of the ramp, paying no attention to him, and dimly and as though from a great distance he had heard him refuse to kill him. He had heard, but he did not comprehend. He expected to be killed, for such was the custom and the law of the arena. He had sought to kill this man; he would have shown him no mercy; so he could not understand the mercy of Tarzan's indifference that had been extended to him.

Phobeg's bloodshot eyes wandered helplessly about the arena, seeking nothing or no one in particular; sympathy was not to be found there, nor mercy, nor any friend; such were not for the vanquished. The frenzied blood-lust of the mob fascinated him. A few minutes ago it had been acclaiming him; now it condemned him to death. His gaze reached the royal loge as Erot leaned far out and shouted to Tarzan standing below.

"Kill him, fellow!" he cried. "It is the Queen's command."

Phobeg's eyes dropped to the figure of the ape-man, and he braced himself for a final effort to delay the inevitable. He knew that he had met one mightier than himself and that he must die when the other wished; but the law of self-preservation compelled him to defend himself, however hopelessly.

The ape-man glanced up at the Queen's favorite. "Tarzan kills only whom it pleases him to kill." He spoke in a low voice that yet carried to the royal loge. "I shall not kill Phobeg."

"You fool," cried Erot, "do you not understand that it is the Queen's wish, that it is the Queen's command, which no one may disobey and live, that you kill the fellow?"

"If the Queen wants him killed, why doesn't she send you down to do it? She is your Queen, not mine." There was neither awe nor respect in the voice of the ape-man.

Erot looked horrified. He glanced at the Queen. "Shall I order the guard to destroy the impudent savage?" he asked.

Nemone shook her head. Her countenance remained inscrutable, but a strange light burned in her eyes. "We give them both their lives," she said. "Set Phobeg free, and bring the other to me in the palace"; then she rose as a sign that the games were over.

Many miles to the south of the Field of the Lions in the valley of Onthar a lion moved restlessly just within the confines of a forest. He paced rapidly first in one direction and then in another; his movements were erratic; sometimes his nose was near the ground and, again, it was in the air as though he were searching for something or some one. Once he raised his head and lifted his great voice in a roar that shook the earth and sent Manu, the monkey, fleeing through the trees with his brothers and sisters. In the distance a bull elephant trumpeted, and then silence fell once more upon the jungle.

10

In the Palace of the Queen

A DETACHMENT of common warriors commanded by an under-officer had escorted Tarzan to the stadium, but he returned to the city in the company of nobles. Several of them had clustered about him immediately following the gesture of Nemone that had suggested to them that this stranger might be the recipient of further royal favors.

Congratulating him upon his victory, praising his prowess, asking innumerable questions, they followed him from the arena, and at the top of the ramp another noble accosted him. It was Gemnon.

"The Queen has commanded me to accompany you to the city and look after you," he explained. "This evening I am to bring you to her in the palace; but in the meantime you will want to bathe and rest, and I imagine that you might welcome some decent food after the prison fare you have been eating recently."

"I shall be glad of a bath and good food," replied Tarzan, "but why should I rest? I have been doing nothing else for several days."

"But you have just come through a terrific battle for your life!" exclaimed Gemnon. "You must be tired."

Tarzan shrugged his broad shoulders. "Perhaps you had better look after Phobeg instead," he replied. "It is he who needs rest; I am not tired."

Gemnon laughed. "Phobeg should consider himself lucky to be alive. If any one looks after him it will be himself."

They were walking toward the city now. The other nobles

had joined their own parties or had dropped behind, and Gemnon and Tarzan were alone, if two may be said to be alone who are surrounded by a chattering mob through which bodies of armed men and lion-drawn chariots are making their slow way. Those near Tarzan were discussing him animatedly, but because of the nobles they kept their distance from him. They commented upon his giant strength and the deceptive appearance of his muscular development, the flowing symmetry of which scarce proclaimed the titanic power of the steel thews of the lord of the jungle.

"You are popular now," commented Gemnon.

"A few minutes ago they were screaming at Phobeg to kill me," Tarzan reminded him.

"I am really surprised that they are so friendly," remarked Gemnon. "You cheated them of a death—the one thing they are all hoping and praying to see when they go to the stadium. It is for this they pay their lepta for admission. Also, most of them lost more money betting on Phobeg; but those who won on you should love you, for they won much; the odds were as high as one hundred to one against you.

"It is the nobles, though, who have the greatest grievance against you," continued Gemnon, grinning. "Several of them lost their entire fortunes. Those closest to Nemone always have to cover her bets; and, believing that she would bet on Phobeg, they placed large bets on him among the audience to cover their losses to Nemone; then Nemone insisted upon betting on you, and they had to bet more money on Phobeg —ten million drachmas to cover Nemone's hundred thousand. I estimate that that one small group lost close to twenty million drachmas."

"And Nemone won ten million?" asked Tarzan.

"Yes," replied Gemnon; "which may account for the fact that you are alive now."

"Why should I not be alive?"

"You flouted the Queen; before thousands of her people you refused to obey her direct command. No, not even the ten million drachmas can account for it; there is some other reason why Nemone spared you. Perhaps she is contemplating for you a death that will give her greater satisfaction. Knowing Nemone as I do, I cannot believe that she will let you live; she would not be Nemone if she forgave so serious an affront to her majesty."

"Phobeg was going to kill me," Tarzan reminded him.

"But Nemone is not Phobeg. Nemone is Queen, and——"

"And what?" asked the ape-man.

Gemnon shrugged. "I was thinking aloud, which is a bad habit for one who enjoys life. Doubtless you may live long enough to know her better than you do now and then you can do your own thinking—but do not do it aloud."

"Did you lose much on Phobeg?" inquired Tarzan.

"I won; I bet on you. I met one of Erot's slaves who was going to place some of his master's money on Phobeg; I took it all. You know I had seen a little more of you than the other nobles and I believed that you had a chance, but I was backing your intelligence and agility against Phobeg's strength, stupidity, and awkwardness; even I did not dream that you were stronger than he."

"And the odds were good!"

Gemnon smiled. "Too good to be overlooked; it was more than a reasonable gamble. But I cannot understand Nemone; she is a great bettor but no gambler. She always puts her money on the favorite, and may Thoos help him if he does not win."

"A woman's intuition," suggested the ape-man.

"I think not; Nemone is too practical and calculating to act on intuition alone; she had some other reason. What it is, none knows but Nemone. The same mysterious motivation saved your life today or, perhaps I should say, prolonged it."

"I am going to see her this evening," said Tarzan, "and doubtless I shall affront her again; it seems that I have done so both times that I have seen her."

"Do not forget that she practically sentenced you to death for the first offense," Gemnon reminded him. "At that time she must have been certain that Phobeg would kill you. If I were you I should not annoy her."

When they reached the city, Gemnon took Tarzan to his own quarters in the palace. These consisted of a bedroom and bath in addition to a living room that was shared with another officer. Here Tarzan found the usual decorations of weapons, shields, and mounted heads in addition to pictures painted on leather. He saw no books, nor any other printed matter; neither was there any sign of writing materials in the rooms. He wanted to question Gemnon on this subject, but he found that he had never learned any word for writing or for a written language.

The bath interested the ape-man. The tub was a coffinlike affair made of clay and baked; the plumbing fixtures were apparently all of solid gold. While questioning Gemnon he learned that the water was brought from the mountains east of the city through clay pipes of considerable size and distributed by means of pressure tanks distributed throughout all of urban Cathne.

Gemnon summoned a slave to prepare the bath, and when Tarzan had finished, a meal was awaiting him in the living room. While he was eating, and Gemnon lounged near in conversation, another young noble entered the apartment. He had a narrow face and rather unpleasant eyes, nor was he overly cordial when Gemnon introduced him to Tarzan.

"Xerstle and I are quartered together," Gemnon explained.

"I have orders to move out," snapped Xerstle.

"Why is that?" asked Gemnon.

"To make room for your friend here," replied Xerstle sourly, and then he went into his own room mumbling something about slaves and savages.

"He does not seem pleased," remarked Tarzan.

"But I am," replied Gemnon in a low voice. "Xerstle and I have not gotten along well together. We have nothing in common. He is one of Erot's friends and was elevated from nothing after Erot became Nemone's favorite. He is the son of a foreman at the mines. If they had elevated his father he would have been an acquisition to the nobility, for he is a splendid man; but Xerstle is a rat—like his friend, Erot."

"I have heard something of your nobility," said Tarzan; "I understand that there are two classes of nobles, and that one class rather looks upon the other with contempt even though a man of the lower class may hold a higher title than many of those in the other class."

"We do not look upon them with contempt if they are worthy men," replied Gemnon. "The old nobility, the Lion Men of Cathne, is hereditary; the other is but temporary—for the lifetime of the man who has received it as a special mark of favor from the throne. In one respect at least it reflects greater glory on its possessor than does hereditary nobility, as it is often the deserved reward of merit. I am a noble by accident of birth; had I not been born a noble I

might never have become one. I am a lion man because my
father was; I may own lions because, beyond the memory of
man, an ancient ancestor of mine led the king's lions to battle."

"What did Erot do to win his patent of nobility?" inquired
the ape-man.

Gemnon grimaced. "Whatever services he has rendered
have been personal; he has never served the state with distinction. If he owns any distinction, it is that of being the
prince of flatterers, the king of sycophants."

"Your Queen seems too intelligent a woman to be duped
by flattery."

"No one is, always."

"There are no sycophants among the beasts," said Tarzan.

"What do you mean by that?" demanded Gemnon. "Erot
is almost a beast."

"You malign the beasts. Did you ever see a lion that
fawned upon another creature to curry favor?"

"But beasts are different," argued Gemnon.

"Yes; they have left all the petty meannesses to man."

"You do not think very highly of men."

"None does who thinks, who compares them with the
beasts."

"We are what we are born," rejoined Gemnon; "some are
beasts, some are men, and some are men who behave like
beasts."

"But none, thank God, are beasts that behave like men,"
retorted Tarzan, smiling.

Xerstle, entering from his room, interrupted their conversation. "I have gathered my things together," he said; "I
shall send a slave for them presently." His manner was short
and brusque. Gemnon merely nodded in assent, and Xerstle
departed.

"He does not seem pleased," commented the ape-man.

"May Xarator have him!" ejaculated Gemnon; "though
he would serve a better purpose as food for my lions," he
added as an afterthought; "if they would eat him."

"You own lions?" inquired Tarzan.

"Certainly," replied Gemnon. "I am a lion man and must
own lions. It is a caste obligation. Each lion man must own
lions of war to fight in the service of the Queen. I have five.

In times of peace I use them for hunting and racing. Only royalty and the lion men may own lions."

The sun was setting behind the mountains that rimmed the western edge of the Field of the Lions as a slave entered the apartment with a lighted cresset which he hung at the end of a chain depending from the ceiling.

"It is time for the evening meal," announced Gemnon, rising.

"I have eaten," replied Tarzan.

"Come anyway; it may interest you to meet the other nobles of the palace."

Tarzan arose. "Very well," he said and followed Gemnon from the apartment.

Forty nobles were assembled in a large dining room on the main floor of the palace as Gemnon and Tarzan entered. Tomos was there and Erot and Xerstle; several of the others Tarzan also recognized as having been seen by him before either in the council room or at the stadium. A sudden silence fell upon the assemblage as he entered, as though the men had been interrupted while discussing either him or Gemnon.

"This is Tarzan," announced Gemnon by way of introduction as he led the ape-man to the table.

Tomos, who sat at the head of the table, did not appear pleased. Erot was scowling; it was he who spoke first. "This table is for nobles," he said, "not for slaves."

"By his own prowess and the grace of her majesty, the Queen, this man is here as my guest," said Gemnon quietly. "If one of my equals takes exception to his presence, I will be glad to discuss the matter with swords," and then he turned to Tarzan. "Because this man sits at table with nobles of my own rank I apologize for the inference he intended you to draw from his words. I hope you are not offended."

"Does the jackal offend the lion?" asked the ape-man.

The meal was not a complete success socially. Erot and Xerstle whispered together. Tomos did not speak but applied himself assiduously to the business of eating. Several of Gemnon's friends engaged Tarzan in conversation; and he found one or two of them agreeable, but others were inclined to be patronizing. Possibly they would have been surprised and their attitude toward him different had they known that their guest was a peer of England, but then again this might have made little impression upon them inasmuch as none of them had ever heard of England. However, Tarzan did not enlighten them. He did not care what they thought, and so the meal progressed with many silences.

When Tomos arose and the others were free to go, Gemnon conducted Tarzan to the apartments of the Queen after returning to his own apartments to don a more elaborate habergeon, helmet, and equipment.

"Do not forget to kneel when we enter the presence of Nemone," cautioned Gemnon, "and do not speak until she addresses you."

A noble received them in a small anteroom where he left them while he went to announce their presence to the Queen, and as they waited Gemnon's eyes watched the tall stranger standing quietly near him.

"Have you no nerves?" he asked presently.

"What do you mean?" demanded the ape-man.

"I have seen the bravest warriors tremble who had been summoned before Nemone," explained his companion.

"I have never trembled," replied Tarzan. "How is it done?"

"Perhaps Nemone will teach you to tremble."

"Perhaps, but why should I tremble to go where a jackal does not tremble to go?"

"I do not understand what you mean by that," said Gemnon puzzled.

"Erot is in there."

Gemnon grinned. "But how do you know that?" he asked.

"I know," said Tarzan; he did not think it necessary to explain that when the noble had opened the door his sensitive nostrils had caught the scent spoor of the Queen's favorite.

"I hope not," said Gemnon, an expression of concern upon his countenance. "If he is there this may be a trap from which you will never come out alive."

"One might fear the Queen," replied Tarzan, "but not the jackal."

"It is the Queen of whom I was thinking."

The noble returned to the anteroom. He nodded to Tarzan. "Her majesty will receive you now," he said. "You may go, Gemnon; your attendance will not be required." Then he turned to the ape-man once more. "When I open the door and announce you, enter the room and kneel. Remain kneeling until the Queen tells you to arise, and do not speak until after her majesty addresses you. Do you hear?"

"I hear," replied Tarzan. "Open the door!"

Gemnon, just leaving the anteroom by another doorway, heard and smiled; but the noble did not smile. He frowned. The bronzed giant had spoken to him in a tone of command, but the noble did not know what to do about it; so he opened the door. But he got some revenge, or at least he thought that he did.

"The slave, Tarzan!" he announced in a loud voice.

The lord of the jungle stepped into the adjoining chamber, crossed to the center of it, and stood erect, silently regarding Nemone. He did not kneel. Erot was there standing at the foot of a couch upon which the Queen reclined upon fat pillows. The Queen regarded Tarzan from her deep eyes without any change of expression, but Erot scowled angrily.

"Kneel, you fool!" he commanded.

"Silence!" admonished Nemone. "It is I who give commands."

Erot flushed and fingered the golden hilt of his sword. Tarzan neither spoke nor moved nor took his eyes from the eyes of Nemone. Though he had thought her beautiful before, he realized now that she was even more gorgeous than he had believed it possible for any woman to be.

"I shall not need you again tonight, Erot," said Nemone; "you may go now."

Now Erot paled and then turned fiery red. He started to speak but thought better of it; then he backed to the doorway, executed a bow that brought him to one knee, arose, and departed.

As Tarzan had crossed the threshold his observing eyes had noted every detail of the room's interior almost in a single, sweeping glance. The chamber was not large, but it was magnificent in its conception and its appointments. Columns of solid gold supported the ceiling, the walls were tiled with ivory, the floor a mosaic of colored stones upon which were scattered rugs of colored stuff and the skins of animals, among which was one that attracted the ape-man's instant attention—the skin of a man tanned with the head on.

On the walls were paintings, for the most part very crude, and the usual array of heads of animals and men, and at one end of the room a great lion was chained between two of the golden Doric columns. He was a very large lion with a tuft of white hair in his mane directly in the center of the back of his neck. From the instant that Tarzan entered the room the lion eyed him malevolently, and Erot had scarcely passed out and closed the door behind him when the beast sprang to his feet with a terrific roar and leaped at the ape-man. The chains stopped him and he dropped down, growling.

"Belthar does not like you," said Nemone who had remained unmoved when the beast sprang. She noticed, too, that Tarzan had not started nor given any other indication that he had heard the lion or seen him; and she was pleased.

"He but reflects the attitude of all Cathne," replied Tarzan.

"That is not true," contradicted Nemone.

"No?"

"*I* like you." Nemone's voice was low and caressing. "You defied me before my people at the stadium today, but I did not have you destroyed. Do you suppose that I should have permitted you to live if I had not liked you? You do not kneel to me. No one else in the world has ever refused to do that and lived. I have never seen a man like you. I do not understand you. I am beginning to think that I do not understand myself. The leopard does not become a sheep in a few hours, yet it seems to me that I have changed as much as that since I first saw you; but that is not solely because I like you; I think that it is more because there is something mysterious about you that I cannot fathom. You have piqued my curiosity."

"And when that is satisfied you will kill me, perhaps?" asked Tarzan, a half smile curving his lip.

"Perhaps," admitted Nemone with a low laugh. "Come here and sit down beside me; I want to talk with you; I want to know more about you."

"I shall see that you do not learn too much," Tarzan assured her as he crossed to the couch and seated himself facing her, while Belthar growled and strained at his chains.

"In your own country you are no slave," said Nemone; "but I do not need to ask that; your every act has proved it. Perhaps you are a king?"

Tarzan shook his head. "I am Tarzan," he said, as though that explained everything, setting him above kings.

"Are you a lion man? You *must* be," insisted the Queen.

"It would not make me better nor worse; so what difference does it make? You might make Erot a king, but he would still be Erot."

A sudden frown darkened Nemone's countenance. "What do you mean by that?" she demanded. There was a suggestion of anger in her tone.

"I mean that a title of nobility does not make a man noble, that you may call a jackal a lion; but he will still be a jackal."

"Do you not know that I am supposed to be very fond of Erot," she demanded, "or that you may drive my patience too far?"

Tarzan shrugged. "You show execrable taste."

Nemone sat up very straight. Her eyes flashed. "I should have you killed!" she cried. Tarzan said nothing. He just kept his eyes on hers. She could not tell whether or not he was laughing at her. Finally she sank back on her pillows with a gesture of resignation. "What is the use?" she demanded. "You probably would not let me get any satisfaction from killing you anyway, and by this time I should be accustomed to being affronted."

"What you are not accustomed to is hearing the truth. Everyone is afraid of you. The reason you are interested in me is because I am not. It might do you good to hear the truth more often."

"For instance?"

"I am not going to undertake the thankless job of regenerating royalty," Tarzan assured her with a laugh.

"Let us stop quarreling. Nemone forgives you."

"I do not quarrel," said Tarzan; "only the weak and the wrong quarrel."

"Now answer my question. Are you a lion man in your own country?"

"I am a noble," replied the ape-man, "but I can tell you that that means little; a ditch digger may become a noble if he control enough votes, or a rich brewer if he subscribe a large amount of money to the political party in power."

"And which were you," demanded Nemone, "a ditch digger or a rich brewer?"

"Neither," laughed Tarzan.

"Then why are you a noble?" insisted the Queen.

"For even less reason than either of those," admitted the ape-man. "I am a noble through no merit of my own but by an accident of birth; my family for many generations has been noble."

"Ah!" exclaimed Nemone. "It is just as I thought; you *are* a lion man!"

"And what of it?" demanded Tarzan.

"It simplifies matters," she explained, but she did not amplify the explanation nor did Tarzan either understand or inquire as to its implication. As a matter of fact he was not greatly interested in the subject.

Nemone extended a hand and laid it on his, a soft, warm hand that trembled just a little. "I am going to give you your freedom," she said, "but on one condition."

"And what is that?" asked the ape-man.

"That you remain here, that you do not try to leave Onthar—or me." Her voice was eager and just a little husky, as though she spoke under suppressed emotion.

Tarzan remained silent. He would not promise, and so he did not speak. He realized, too, how easy it would be to remain if Nemone bid one do so. She fascinated him; she seemed to exercise a subtle influence, mysterious, hypnotic; yet he was determined to make no promise.

"I will make you a noble of Cathne," whispered Nemone. She was sitting erect now, her face close to Tarzan's. He could feel the warmth of her body close to his; the aura of some exotic scent was in his nostrils; her fingers closed upon his arm with a fierceness that hurt. "I will have made for you helmets of gold and habergeons of ivory, the most magnificent in Cathne; I will give you lions, fifty, a hundred; you shall be the richest, the most powerful noble of my court!"

The lord of the jungle felt weak beneath the spell of her burning eyes. "I do not want *such* things," he said.

Her soft arm crept up about his neck. A tender light, that was new to them, welled in the eyes of Nemone, the Queen of Cathne. "Tarzan!" she whispered.

And then a door at the far end of the chamber opened and a negress entered. She had been very tall, but now she was old and bent; her scraggly wool was scant and white. Her withered lips were twisted into something that might have been either a snarl or a grin, revealing her toothless gums. She stood in the doorway leaning upon a staff and shaking her head, an ancient, palsied hag.

At the interruption Nemone straightened and looked around. The expression that had transformed and softened her countenance was swept away by a sudden wave of rage, inarticulate but no less terrible.

The old hag tapped upon the floor with her staff; her head nodded ceaselessly like that of some grotesque and horrible doll, and her lips were still contorted in what Tarzan realized now was no smile but a hideous snarl. "Come!" she cackled. "Come! Come! Come!"

Nemone sprang to her feet and faced the woman. "M'duze!" she screamed. "I could kill you! I could tear you to pieces! Get out of here!"

But the old woman only tapped with her staff and cackled, "Come! Come! Come!"

Slowly Nemone approached her. As one drawn by an invisible and irresistible power the Queen crossed the chamber, the old hag stepped aside, and the Queen passed on through the doorway into the darkness of a corridor beyond. The old woman turned her eyes upon Tarzan, and, snarling, backed through the doorway after Nemone. Noiselessly the door closed behind them.

Tarzan had arisen as Nemone arose. For an instant he hesitated and then took a step toward the doorway in pursuit of the Queen and the old hag; then he heard a door open and a step behind him, and turned to see the noble who had ushered him into Nemone's presence standing just within the threshold.

"You may return to the quarters of Gemnon," announced the noble politely.

Tarzan shook himself as might a lion; he drew a palm across his eyes as one whose vision has been clouded by a mist; then he drew a deep sigh and moved toward the doorway as the noble stepped aside to let him pass, but whether it was a sigh of relief or regret, who may say?

As the lord of the jungle passed out of the chamber, Belthar sprang to the ends of his chains with a thunderous roar.

11

The Lions of Cathne

WHEN Gemnon entered the living room of their quarters the morning after Tarzan's audience with Nemone, he found the ape-man standing by the window looking out over the palace grounds.

"I am glad to see you here this morning," said the Cathnean.

"And surprised, perhaps," suggested the lord of the jungle.

"I should not have been surprised had you never returned," replied Gemnon. "How did she receive you? And Erot? I suppose he was glad to have you there!"

Tarzan smiled. "He did not appear to be, but it did not matter much as the Queen sent him away immediately."

"And you were alone with her all evening?" Gemnon appeared incredulous.

"Belthar and I," Tarzan corrected him. "Belthar does not seem to like me any better than Erot does."

"Yes, Belthar would be there," commented Gemnon. "She usually has him chained near her. But do not be offended if he does not like you; Belthar likes no one. Perhaps I should qualify that by saying that he likes no one alive, for he is very fond of dead men. Belthar is a man-eater. How did Nemone treat you?"

"She was gracious," Tarzan assured him, "and that, too, notwithstanding the fact that the first thing that I did offended her royal majesty."

"And what was that?" demanded Gemnon.

"I remained standing when I should have kneeled," explained Tarzan.

"But I told you to kneel," exclaimed Gemnon.

"So did the noble at the door."

"And you forgot?"

"No."

"You refused to kneel? and she did not have you destroyed! It is incredible."

"But it is true, and she offered to make me a noble and give me a hundred lions."

Gemnon shook his head. "What enchantment have you worked to so change Nemone?"

"None; it was I who was under a spell. I have told you these things because I do not understand them. You are the only friend I have in Cathne, and I come to you for an explanation of much that was mysterious in my visit to the Queen last night; I doubt that I or another can ever understand the woman herself. She can be tender or terrible, weak or strong within the span of a dozen seconds. One moment she is the autocrat, the next the obedient vassal of a slave."

"Ah!" exclaimed Gemnon; "so you saw M'duze! I'll warrant she was none too cordial."

"No," admitted the ape-man. "As a matter of fact she did not pay any attention to me; she just ordered Nemone out of the room, and Nemone went. The remarkable feature of the occurrence lies in the fact that, though the Queen did not want to leave and was very angry about it, she obeyed the old black woman meekly."

"There are many legends surrounding M'duze," said Gemnon; "but there is one that is whispered more often than the others, though you may rest assured that it is only whispered and, at that, only among trusted friends.

"M'duze has been a slave in the royal family since the days of Nemone's grandfather; she was only a child then, a few years older than the King's son, Nemone's father. The oldsters recall that she was a fine-looking young negress, and the legend that is only whispered is that Nemone is her daughter.

"About a year after Nemone was born, in the tenth year of her father's reign, the Queen died under peculiar and suspicious circumstances just before she was to have been confined. The child, a son, was born just before the Queen expired. He was named Alextar, and he still lives."

"Then why is he not king?" demanded Tarzan.

"That is a long story of mystery and court intrigue and murder, perhaps, of which more is surmised than is actually known by more than two now living. Perhaps Nemone knows, but that is doubtful though she must guess close to the truth.

"Immediately following the death of the Queen the influence of M'duze increased and became more apparent. M'duze favored Tomos, a noble of little or no importance at the time; and from that day the influence and power of Tomos grew. Then, about a year after the death of the Queen, the King died. It was so obvious that he had been poisoned that a revolt of the nobles was barely averted; but Tomos, guided by M'duze, conciliated them by fixing the guilt upon a slave woman of whom M'duze was jealous and executing her.

"For ten years Tomos ruled as regent for the boy, Alextar. During this time he had, quite naturally, established his own following in important positions in the palace and in the council. Alextar was adjudged insane and imprisoned in the temple; Nemone, at the age of twelve, was crowned Queen of Cathne.

"Erot is a creature of M'duze and Tomos, a situation that has produced a *contretemps* that would be amusing were it not so tragic. Tomos wishes to marry Nemone, but M'duze will not permit it, and, if another theory is correct, her objection is well grounded. This theory is that Tomos, and not the old king, is the father of Nemone. M'duze wishes Nemone to marry Erot, but Erot is not a lion man, and, so far, the Queen has refused to break this ancient custom that requires the ruler to marry into this highest class of Cathneans.

"M'duze is insistent upon the marriage because she can control Erot; and she discourages any interest which Nemone may manifest in other men, which undoubtedly accounts for her having interrupted the Queen's visit with you.

"You may rest assured that M'duze is your enemy, and it may be of value to you to recall that whoever has stood in the old hag's path has died a violent death. Beware of M'duze and Tomos and Erot; and, as a friend, I may say to you in confidence, beware of Nemone, also. And now let us forget the cruel and sordid side of Cathne and go for that walk I promised you for this morning that you may see the beauty of the city and the riches of her citizens."

Along avenues bordered by old trees Gemnon led Tarzan between the low, white and gold homes of nobles, glimpses of which were discernible only occasionally through grilled gateways in the walls that enclosed their spacious grounds. For a mile they walked along the stone-flagged street. Passing nobles greeted Gemnon, some nodding to his companion; artizans, tradesmen, and slaves stopped to stare at the strange, bronzed giant who had overthrown the strongest man in Cathne.

Then they came to a high wall that separated this section of the city from the next. Massive gates, swung wide now and guarded by warriors, opened into a portion of the city inhabited by better class artizans and tradesmen. Their grounds were less spacious, their houses smaller and plainer; but evidences of prosperity and even affluence were apparent everywhere.

Beyond this was a meaner district, yet even here all was orderly and neat, nor was there any sign of abject poverty in either the people or their homes. Here, as in the other portions of the city, they occasionally met a tame lion either wandering about or lying before the gate of its master's grounds.

Presently the ape-man's attention was attracted by a lion a short distance ahead of them; the beast was lying on the body of a man which it was devouring.

"Your streets do not seem to be entirely safe for pedestrians," commented the lord of the jungle, indicating the feeding lion with a nod of the head.

Gemnon laughed. "You notice that the pedestrians do not seem to be much concerned," he replied, calling attention to the people passing to and fro past the lion and its prey, merely turning aside enough to avoid them. "The lions must eat."

"Do they kill many of your citizens?"

"Very few. The man you see there died, and his corpse was thrown into the street for the lions. The lion did not kill him. You see he is naked; that shows that he was dead before the lion got him. When a person dies, if there be no one who can or will pay for a funeral cortege, the body is disposed of in this way if not diseased; those who die of disease and those whose relatives can afford a funeral cortege find their last resting place in Xarator, though there are also many of the latter that are thrown to the lions by preference. You know we think a great deal of lions here in Cathne, and it is no disgrace but rather the contrary to be devoured by one. You see, our god is a lion."

"Do the lions eat human flesh exclusively?" inquired Tarzan.

"No. We hunt sheep, goats, and elephants in Thenar to provide them with food when there is not enough human flesh to keep them well fed, for we must keep them from hunger if we are to prevent them turning man-eaters."

"Then they never kill men for food?"

"Oh, yes, occasionally; but a lion that develops that habit is destroyed; and, after all, only a few old pets are turned loose in the streets. There are about five hundred lions inside the city, and all but a few of these are kept in enclosures on their owners' property. The best racing and hunting lions are kept in private stables.

"The Queen has fully three hundred full grown males; these are the war lions. Some of the Queen's lions are trained for racing and some for hunting; she likes to hunt, and now that the rainy season is over the hunting lions of Nemone will doubtless soon be in the field."

"Where do you get all these lions?" asked the ape-man.

"We raise them ourselves," explained Gemnon. "Outside the city is a breeding plant where the females are kept. It is maintained by Nemone, and each lion man who owns females pays a stipulated sum for their keep. We raise a great many lions, for there are many killed each year in hunting, during raids, and in war. You see, we hunt elephants with them; and in these hunts many lions are killed. The Atheneans also kill a number each year when we take our lions into Thenar to hunt or raid, and quite a few escape. Most of these are still running wild in the valley or in Thenar, and there are some wild lions that have come in from the mountains. All of these are very ferocious."

As they talked they continued on toward the center of the city until they came to a large square that was bounded on all sides by shops. Here were many people. All classes from nobles to slaves mingled before the shops and in the great open square of the market place. There were lions held by slaves who were exhibiting them for sale for their noble masters who dickered with prospective purchasers, other nobles.

Near the lion market was the slave block; and as slaves, unlike lions, might be owned by anyone, there was brisk bidding on the part of many wishing to buy. A huge, black Galla was on the block as Tarzan and Gemnon paused to watch the scene. The man was entirely naked that the buyers might examine him for blemishes; his expression was one of unconcern ordinarily, though occasionally he shot a venomous glance at the owner who was expatiating upon his virtues.

"For all the interest he shows," remarked Tarzan, "one might think that being sold like a piece of merchandise or a bullock was a daily occurrence in his life."

"Not quite daily," replied Gemnon "but no novelty. He has been sold many times. I know him well; I used to own him."

"Look at him!" shouted the seller. "Look at those arms; look at those legs; look at that back! He is as strong as an elephant, and not a blemish on him. Sound as a lion's tooth he is; never ill a day in his life. And docile! a child can handle him."

"He is so refractory that no one can handle him," commented Gemnon in a whisper to the ape-man. "That is the reason I had to get rid of him; that is the reason he is up for sale so often."

"There seem to be plenty of customers interested in him," observed Tarzan.

"Do you see that slave in the red tunic?" asked Gemnon. "He belongs to Xerstle, and he is bidding on that fellow. He knows all about him, too; he knew him when the man belonged to me."

"Then why does he want to buy him?" asked the ape-man.

"I do not know, but there are other uses to which a slave may be put than labor. Xerstle may not care what sort of a disposition the fellow has or even whether he will work. If he owned lions I might think that he was buying the fellow for lion food as he will probably go cheap."

It was Xerstle's slave who bought the Galla as Tarzan and Gemnon moved on to look at the goods displayed in the shops. There were many articles of leather, wood, ivory, or gold; there were dagger-swords, spears, shields, habergeons, helmets, and sandals. One shop displayed nothing but articles of apparel for women; another, perfumes and incense; there were jewelry shops, vegetable shops, and meat shops. The last displayed dried meats and fish and carcasses of goats and sheep. The fronts of these shops were heavily barred to prevent passing lions from raiding them, Gemnon explained.

Wherever Tarzan went he attracted attention; and a small crowd always followed him, for he had been recognized the moment that he had entered the market place. Boys and girls clustered about him gazing at him admiringly, and men and women who had been at the stadium the previous day told those who had not how this stranger giant had lifted Phobeg above his head and hurled him up among the audience.

"Let's get out of here," suggested the lord of the jungle; "I do not like crowds."

"Suppose we go back to the palace and look at the Queen's lions," said Gemnon.

"I would rather look at lions than people," Tarzan assured him.

The war lions of Cathne were kept in stables within the royal grounds at a considerable distance from the palace. The building was of stone neatly laid and painted white; in it each lion had his separate cage; and outside were yards surrounded by high stone walls near the tops of which pointed sticks, set close together and inclined downward on the inside of the walls, kept the lions from escaping. In these yards the lions exercised themselves; there was another, larger arena where they were trained by a corps of keepers under the supervision of nobles; here the racing lions were broken to harness and the hunting lions taught to obey the commands of the hunter, to trail, to charge, to retrieve.

As Tarzan entered the stable a familiar scent spoor impinged upon his nostrils. "Belthar is here," he remarked to Gemnon.

"It is possible," replied the noble, "but I don't understand how you know it."

As they were walking along in front of the cages inspecting the lions that were inside, Gemnon, who was in advance, suddenly halted. "How do you do it?" he demanded. "Last night you knew that Erot was with Nemone, though you could not see him and no one could have informed you; and now you knew that Belthar was here, and, sure enough, he is!"

Tarzan approached and stood beside Gemnon, and the instant that Belthar's eyes fell upon him the beast leaped against the bars of his cage in an effort to seize the ape-man, at the same time voicing an angry roar that shook the building.

Instantly keepers came running to the spot, certain that something had gone amiss; but Gemnon assured them that it was only Belthar exhibiting his bad temper.

"He does not like me," said Tarzan.

"If he ever got you, he would make short work of you," said a head keeper.

"It is evident that he would like to," replied the ape-man.

"He is a bad one and a man-killer," said Gemnon after the keepers had departed, "but Nemone will not have him destroyed. Occasionally he is loosed in the palace arena with someone who has incurred Nemone's disfavor; thus she derives pleasure from the sufferings of the culprit.

"Formerly he was her best hunting lion, but the last time he was used he killed four men and nearly escaped. He has already eaten three keepers who ventured into the arena with him, and he will eat more before good fortune rids us of him.

"Nemone is supposed to entertain a superstition that in some peculiar way her life and the life of Belthar are linked by some mysterious, supernatural bond and that when one dies the other must die. Naturally, under the circumstances, it is neither politic nor safe to suggest that she destroy the old devil. It is odd that he has conceived such a violent dislike for you."

"I have met lions before which did not like me," said Tarzan.

"May you never meet Belthar in the open, my friend!"

12

The Man in the Lion Pit

As Tarzan and Gemnon turned away from Belthar's cage a slave approached the ape-man and addressed him. "Nemone, the Queen, commands your presence immediately," he said; "you are to come to the ivory room; the noble Gemnon will wait in the anteroom. These are the commands of Nemone, the Queen."

"What now? I wonder," remarked Tarzan as they walked through the royal grounds toward the palace.

"No one ever knows why he is summoned to an audience with Nemone until he gets there," commented Gemnon; "one may be going to receive an honor or hear his death sentence. Nemone is capricious. She is always bored and always seeking relief from her boredom. Oftentimes she finds strange avenues of escape that makes one wonder if her mind—but no! such thoughts may not even be whispered among friends."

When Tarzan presented himself he was immediately admitted to the ivory room, where he found Nemone and Erot much as he had found them the preceding night. Nemone greeted him with a smile that was almost pathetically eager; but Erot only scowled darkly, making no effort to conceal his hatred.

"We are having a diversion this morning," Nemone explained, "and we summoned you and Gemnon to enjoy it with us. A party raiding in Thenar a day or so ago captured an Athnean noble; we are going to have some sport with him this morning."

Tarzan nodded. He did not understand what she meant, and he was not particularly interested. He was thinking of M'duze and the night before; wondering what was in the mind of the strange, fascinating woman before him.

Nemone turned to Erot. "Go and tell them we are ready," she directed, "and ascertain if all is in readiness for us."

Erot flushed and backed toward the door, still scowling. "And you need not hurry," added the Queen; "we are not impatient to witness the entertainment. Let them take their time, and be sure to see that all is well ordered."

"It shall be as the Queen commands," replied Erot in a surly tone.

When the door had closed behind him, Nemone motioned Tarzan to a seat upon the couch. "I am afraid that Erot does not like you," she said, smiling. "He is furious that you do not kneel to me, and that I do not compel you to do so. I really do not know, myself, why I do not; but I guess why. Have you not, perhaps, guessed why, too?"

"There might be two reasons, either of which would be sufficient," replied the ape-man.

"And what are they? I have been curious to know how you explained it."

"Consideration of the customs of a stranger and courtesy to a guest," suggested Tarzan.

Nemone considered for a moment. "Yes," she admitted, "either is a fairly good reason, but neither is really in keeping with the customs of the court of Nemone. And then they are practically the same thing; so they constitute only one reason. Is there not another?"

"Yes," replied Tarzan; "there is an even better one; the one which probably influences you to overlook my dereliction."

"And what is it?"

"The fact that you cannot make me kneel."

A hard look flashed in the Queen's eyes; it was not the answer she had been hoping for. Tarzan's eyes did not leave hers; she saw amusement in them. "Oh, why do I endure it!" she cried, and with the query her anger melted. "You should not try to make it so hard for me to be nice to you," she said almost appealingly. "Why do you not meet me half-way? Why are you not nice to me, Tarzan?"

"I wish to be nice to you, Nemone," he replied; "but not

at the price of my self-respect; but that is not the only reason why I shall never kneel to you."

"What is the other reason?" she demanded.

"That I wish you to like me; you would not like me if I cringed to you."

"Perhaps you are right," she admitted musingly. "Everyone cringes, until the sight of it disgusts me; yet I am angry when they do not cringe. Why is that?"

"You will be offended if I tell you," warned the ape-man.

"In the past two days I have become accustomed to being offended," she replied with a grimace of resignation; "so you might as well tell me."

"You are angry if they do not cringe, because you are not quite sure of yourself. You wish this outward evidence of their subservience that you may be constantly reassured that you are Queen of Cathne."

"Who says that I am not Queen of Cathne?" she demanded, instantly on the defensive. "Who says that will find that I am and that I have the power of life and death. If I chose, I could have you destroyed in an instant."

"You do not impress me," said Tarzan. "I have not said that you are not Queen of Cathne, only that your manner may often suggest your own doubts. A queen should be so sure of herself that she can always afford to be gracious and merciful."

For a while Nemone sat in silence, evidently pondering the thought that Tarzan had suggested. "They would not understand," she said at last; "if I were gracious and merciful they would think me weak; then they would take advantage of me; and eventually they would destroy me. You do not know them. But you are different; I can be gracious and merciful to you and you will never try to take advantage of my kindness; you will not misunderstand it.

"Oh, Tarzan, I wish that you would promise to remain in Cathne. If you will, there is nothing that you may not have from Nemone. I would build you a palace second only to my own. I would be very good to you; we—you could be very happy here."

The ape-man shook his head. "Tarzan can be happy in the jungle only."

Nemone leaned close to him; she seized him fiercely

by the shoulders. "I will make you happy here," she whispered passionately. "You do not know Nemone. Wait! The time will come when you will want to stay—for me!"

"Erot and M'duze and Tomos may think differently," Tarzan reminded her.

"I hate them!" cried Nemone. "If they interfere this time, I shall kill them all; this time I shall have my own way; she shall not rob me of all happiness. But do not speak of her; never speak her name to me again. And as for Erot," she snapped her fingers. "I crush a worm beneath my sandal, and no one misses it. No one would miss Erot, least of all I; I have long been tired of him. He is a stupid, egotistical fool; but he is better than nothing."

The door opened and Erot entered unceremoniously; he kneeled, but the act was nearer a gesture than an accomplished fact. Nemone flashed an angry look at him.

"Before you enter our presence," she said coldly, "see to it that you are properly announced and that we have expressed a desire to receive you."

"But your majesty," objected Erot, "have I not been in the habit of——"

"You have gotten into bad habits," she interrupted; "see that you mend them. Is the diversion arranged?"

"All is in readiness, your majesty," replied the crestfallen Erot.

"Come, then!" directed Nemone, motioning Tarzan to follow her.

In the anteroom they found Gemnon waiting, and the Queen bid him accompany them. Preceded and followed by armed guards, the three passed along several corridors and through a number of rooms, then up a stairway to the second floor of the palace. Here they were conducted to a balcony overlooking a small enclosed court. The windows opening onto this court from the first story of the building were heavily barred; and from just below the top of the parapet, behind which the Queen and her party sat, sharpened stakes protruded, giving the court the appearance of a miniature arena for wild animals.

As Tarzan looked down into the courtyard, wondering a little what the nature of the diversion was to be, a door at one end swung open and a young lion stepped out into the sunlight, blinking his eyes and looking about. When he saw those on the balcony looking down at him, he growled.

"He is going to make a good lion," remarked Nemone. "From a cub, he has always been vicious."

"What is he doing in here?" asked Tarzan, "or what is he going to do?"

"He is going to entertain us," replied Nemone. "Presently an enemy of Cathne will be turned into the pit with him, the Athnean who was captured in Thenar."

"And if he kills the lion you will give him his liberty?" demanded Tarzan.

Nemone laughed. "I promise that I will, but he will not kill the lion."

"He might," said Tarzan; "men have killed lions before."

"With their bare hands?" asked Nemone.

"You mean the man will not be armed?" demanded Tarzan incredulously.

"Why, of course not," exclaimed Nemone. "He is not being put in there to kill or wound a fine young lion but to be killed."

"And he has no chance then! That is not sport; it is murder!"

"Perhaps you would like to go down and defend him," sneered Erot. "The Queen would give the fellow his liberty if he had a champion who would kill the lion, for that is the custom."

"It is a custom that is without a precedent since I have been Queen," said Nemone. "It is true that it is a law of the arena, but I have yet to see a champion volunteer to take the risk."

The lion paced across the courtyard and stood directly beneath the balcony, glaring up at them. He was a splendid beast, young but full-grown.

"He is going to be a mean customer," remarked Gemnon.

"He already is," rejoined the Queen. "I was going to make a racing lion of him, but after he killed a couple of trainers I decided that he would make a better hunting lion for grand hunts. There is the Athnean." She pointed down into the courtyard. "He is a fine-looking young fellow."

Tarzan glanced at the stalwart figure in ivory standing upon the opposite side of the small arena bravely awaiting its fate; then the lion turned its head slowly in the direction of the prey it had not yet seen. At the same instant

Tarzan seized the hilt of Erot's dagger-like sword, tore the weapon from its sheath, and, stepping to the top of the parapet, leaped for the lion below.

So quickly and so silently had he moved that none was aware of his intent until it had been accomplished. Gemnon voiced an ejaculation of astonishment; Erot, of relief; while Nemone cried out in genuine terror and alarm. Leaning over the parapet, the Queen saw the lion struggling to tear the body that had crushed it to the stone flagging or escape from beneath it. The horrid growls of the beast reverberated in the narrow confines of the pit, and mingled with them were the growls of the beast-man on its back. One bronzed arm was about the maned neck of the carnivore, two powerful legs were locked around its middle, and the sharp point of Erot's sword was awaiting the opportune instant to plunge into the savage heart. The Athnean was running toward the two embattled beasts.

"By Thoos!" exclaimed Nemone. "If the lion kills him, I will have it torn limb from limb. It must not kill him! Go down there, Erot, and help him; go, Gemnon!"

Gemnon did not wait, but springing to the parapet, he lowered himself by the stakes and dropped into the court-yard. Erot hung back. "Let him take care of himself," he grumbled.

Nemone turned to the guard standing behind her. She was white with apprehension because of Tarzan and with rage and disgust at Erot. "Throw him into the pit!" she commanded, pointing at the cringing favorite; but Erot did not wait to be thrown, and a moment later he had followed Gemnon to the stone flagging of the courtyard.

Neither Erot nor Gemnon nor the man from Athne were needed to save Tarzan from the lion, for already he had sunk the sword into the tawny side. Twice again the point drove into the wild heart before the roaring beast collapsed upon the white stones, and its great voice was stilled forever.

Then Tarzan rose to his feet. For a moment the men about him, the Queen leaning across the parapet above, the city of gold, all were forgotten. Here was no English lord but a beast of the jungle that had made its kill. With one foot upon the carcass of the lion, the ape-man raised his face toward the heavens, and from the heart of the palace of

Nemone rose the hideous victory cry of the bull ape that has killed.

Gemnon and Erot shuddered, and Nemone drew back in terror; but the Athnean was unmoved; he had heard that savage challenge before. He was Valthor. And now Tarzan turned; all the savagery faded from his countenance as he stretched forth a hand and laid it on Valthor's shoulder. "We meet again, my friend," he said.

"And once again you save my life!" exclaimed the Athnean noble.

The two men had spoken in low tones that had not carried to the ears of Nemone or the others in the balcony; Erot, fearful that the lion might not be dead, had run to the far end of the court, where he was cowering behind a column; that Gemnon might have heard did not concern Tarzan, who trusted the young Cathnean. But those others must not know that he had known Valthor before, or immediately the old story that Tarzan had come from Athne to assassinate Nemone would be revived and then only a miracle could save either of them.

His hand still upon Valthor's shoulder, Tarzan spoke again rapidly in a whisper. "They must not know that we are acquainted," he said. "They are looking for an excuse to kill me, some of them; but as far as you are concerned they do not have to look for any."

Nemone was now calling orders rapidly to those about her. "Go down and let Tarzan out of the arena, Tarzan and Gemnon; send them to me. Erot may go to his quarters until I give further orders; I do not wish to see him again. Take the Athnean back to his cell; later I will decide how he shall be destroyed."

She spoke in the imperious tones of one long accustomed to absolute authority and implicit obedience, and her voice carried plainly to the ears of the men in the arena. It brought the chill of sudden fear to the heart of Erot, who saw his influence waning and recalled tales he had heard of the fate of other royal favorites who had outlived their charm. Into his cunning brain flew a score of schemes to reinstate himself, and each was based upon the elimination of the giant that had supplanted him in the affections of the Queen. He would fly to Tomos, to M'duze; neither of these could afford to see the stranger take Erot's place in the boudoir councils of Nemone and become a power behind the throne.

Tarzan heard the Queen's commands with surprise and resentment, and, wheeling, he looked up at her. "This man is free by your own word," he reminded her. "If he be returned to a cell, I shall go with him, for I have told him that he would be free."

"Do with him as you please," cried Nemone; "he is yours. Only come up to me, Tarzan. I thought that you would be killed, and I am still frightened."

Erot and Gemnon heard these words with vastly different emotions; each recognized that they signalized a change in the affairs of the court of Cathne. Gemnon anticipated the effects of a better influence injected into the councils of Nemone, and was pleased. Erot saw the flimsy structure of his temporary grandeur and reflected authority crumbling to ruin. Both were astonished by this sudden revealment of a new Nemone, whom none had ever before seen bow to the authority of another than M'duze.

Accompanied by Gemnon and Valthor, Tarzan returned to the balcony where Nemone, her composure regained, awaited them. For a moment, moved by excitement and apprehension for Tarzan's safety, she had revealed a feminine side of her character that few of her intimates might even have suspected she possessed; but now she was the Queen again. She surveyed Valthor haughtily and yet with interest.

"What is your name, Athnean?" she demanded.

"Valthor," he replied and added, "of the house of Xanthus."

"We know the house," remarked Nemone; "its head is a king's councillor; a most noble house and close to the royal line in both blood and authority."

"My father is the head of the house of Xanthus," said Valthor.

"Your head would have made a noble trophy for our walls," sighed Nemone, "but we have given our promise that you shall be freed."

"My head would have been honored by a place among your majesty's trophies," replied Valthor, the faintest trace of a smile upon his lips; "but it shall have to be content to wait a more propitious event."

"We shall look forward with keen anticipation to that moment," rejoined Nemone graciously; "but in the meantime we will arrange an escort to return you to Athne, and hope for better fortune the next time that you fall into our hands. Be ready then early tomorrow to return to your own country."

"I thank your majesty," replied Valthor; "I shall be ready, and when I go I shall carry with me, to cherish through life, the memory of the gracious and beautiful Queen of Cathne."

"Our noble Gemnon shall be your host until tomorrow," announced Nemone. "Take him with you now to your quarters, Gemnon, and let it be known that he is Nemone's guest, whom none may harm."

Tarzan would have accompanied Gemnon and Valthor, but Nemone detained him. "You will return to my apartments with me," she directed; "I wish to talk with you."

As they walked through the palace, the Queen did not precede her companion as the etiquette of the court demanded but moved close at his side, looking up into his face as she talked. "I was frightened, Tarzan," she confided. "It is not often that Nemone is frightened by the peril of another, but when I saw you leap into the arena with the lion my heart stood still. Why did you do it, Tarzan?"

"I was disgusted with what I saw," replied the ape-man shortly.

"Disgusted! What do you mean?"

"The cowardliness of the authority that would permit an unarmed and utterly defenseless man to be forced into an arena with a lion," explained Tarzan candidly.

Nemone flushed. "You know that that authority is I," she said coldly.

"Of course I know it," replied the ape-man, "but that only renders it the more odious."

"What do you mean?" she snapped. "Are you trying to drive me beyond my patience? If you knew me better you would know that that is not safe, not even for you, before whom I have already humbled myself."

"I am not seeking to try your patience," replied the ape-man quietly, "for I am neither interested nor concerned in your powers of self-control. I am merely shocked that one so beautiful may at the same time be so heartless. Were you a little more human, Nemone, you would be irresistible."

The flush faded from the Queen's face, the anger from her eyes; she moved on in silence, her mood suddenly introspective; and when they reached the anteroom leading to her private chambers, she halted at the threshold of the latter and laid a hand gently upon the arm of the man at her side.

"You are very brave," she said. "Only a very brave man would have leaped into the arena with the lion to save a stranger; but only the bravest of the brave could have dared to speak to Nemone as you have spoken, for the death that the lion deals may be merciful compared with that which Nemone deals when she has been affronted. Yet perhaps you knew that I would forgive you. Oh, Tarzan, what magic have you exercised to win such power over me!" She took him by the hand then and led him toward the doorway of her chambers. "In here, alone together, you shall teach Nemone how to be human!" As the door swung open there was a new light in the eyes of the Queen of Cathne, a softer light than had ever before shone in those beautiful depths; and then it faded, to be replaced by a cold, hard glitter of bitterness and hate. Facing them, in the center of the apartment, stood M'duze.

She stood there, bent and horrible, wagging her head and tapping the stone floor with her staff. She spoke no word, but fixed them with her baleful glare. As one held in the grip of a power she is unable to resist, Nemone moved slowly toward the ancient hag, leaving Tarzan just beyond the threshold. Slowly and silently the door closed between them. Beyond it the ape-man heard, faintly, the tapping of the staff upon the colored stones of the mosaic.

13

Assassin in the Night

A GREAT lion moved silently from the south across the border of Kaffa. If he were following a trail, the heavy rain that had terminated the wet season must have obliterated it long since; yet he moved on with a certain assurance that betokened no sign of doubt.

Why was he there? What urge had drawn him thus, contrary to the habits and customs of his kind, upon this long and arduous journey? Where was he bound? What or whom did he seek? Only he, Numa, the lion, king of beasts, knew.

In his quarters in the palace, Erot paced the floor, angry and disconsolate. Sprawled on a bench, his feet wide apart, sat Xerstle deep in thought. The two men were facing a crisis, and they were terrified. Had Erot definitely fallen from the favor of the Queen, Xerstle would be dragged down with him; of that there was no doubt.

"But there must be *something* you can do," insisted Xerstle.

"I have seen both Tomos and M'duze," replied Erot wearily, "and they have promised to help. It means as much to them as it does to me. But Nemone is infatuated with this stranger. Even M'duze, who has known her all her life, has never seen her so affected by a passion as now. Even she feels that she may not be able to control the Queen in the face of her mad attachment for the naked barbarian.

"None knows Nemone better than does M'duze, and I can tell you, Xerstle, the old hag is frightened. Nemone hates her, and if the attempted thwarting of this new passion arouses her anger sufficiently it may sweep away the fear that the Queen has already held for M'duze, and she will destroy her. It is this that M'duze fears. And you can imagine how terrified old Tomos is! Without M'duze he would be lost, for Nemone tolerates him only because M'duze demands it."

"But there must be some way," again insisted Xerstle.

"There is no way so long as this fellow, Tarzan, is able to turn Nemone's heart to water," answered Erot. "Why, he does not even kneel to her; and he speaks to her as one might to a naughty slave girl. By the mane of Thoos! I believe that if he kicked her she would like it."

"But there *is* a way!" exclaimed Xerstle in a sudden whisper. "Listen!" and then he launched forth into a detailed explanation of his plan. Erot sat listening to his friend, an expression of rapt interest upon his face. A slave girl came from Xerstle's bedchamber, crossed the living room where the two men talked, and departed into the corridor beyond; but so engrossed were Erot and Xerstle that neither was aware that she had come or that she had gone.

In their quarters that evening Gemnon and Tarzan partook of the final meal of the day, for neither had enjoyed the prospect of again eating with the other nobles. Valthor slept in the bedroom, having asked not to be disturbed until morning.

"When you have definitely displaced Erot conditions will be different," explained Gemnon; "then they will fawn upon you, shower you with attentions, and wait upon your every whim."

"That will never occur," snapped the ape-man.

"Why not?" demanded his companion. "Nemone is mad about you. There is nothing that she would not do for you, absolutely nothing. Why, man, you can rule Cathne if you so choose."

"But I do not choose," replied Tarzan. "Nemone may be mad, but I am not; and even were I, I could never be mad enough to accept a position that had once been filled by Erot. The idea disgusts me; let us talk of something pleasant."

"Very well," consented Gemnon with a smile. "Perhaps I think you are foolish, but I admit that I cannot help but admire your courage and your decency.

"And now for something more pleasant! Something very

much more pleasant! I am going to take you visiting tonight. I am going to take you to see the most beautiful girl in Cathne."

"I thought that there could be no woman in Cathne more beautiful than the Queen," objected Tarzan.

"There would not be if Nemone knew of her," replied Gemnon, "but fortunately she does not know; she has never seen this girl, and may Thoos forbid that she ever does!"

"You are much interested," remarked the ape-man, smiling.

"I am in love with her," explained Gemnon simply.

"And Nemone has never seen her? I should think that a difficult condition to maintain, for Cathne is not large; and if the girl be of the same class as you many other nobles must know of her beauty. One would expect such news to come quickly to the ears of Nemone."

"She is surrounded by very loyal friends, this girl of whom I speak," replied Gemnon. "She is Doria, the daughter of Thudos. Her father is a very powerful noble and head of the faction which wishes to place Alextar on the throne. Only Nemone's knowledge of his great power preserves his life, but owing to the strained relations that exist between Nemone and his house neither he nor members of his family are often at court. Thus it has been easier to prevent knowledge of the great beauty of Doria coming to Nemone."

As the two men were leaving the palace a short time later they came unexpectedly upon Xerstle, who was most effusive in his greetings. "Congratulations, Tarzan!" he exclaimed, halting the companions. "That was a most noble feat you performed in the lion pit today. All the palace is talking about it, and let me be among the first to tell you how glad I am that you have won the confidence of our gracious and beautiful Queen by your bravery, strength, and magnanimity."

Tarzan nodded in acknowledgment of the man's avowal and started to move on, but Xerstle held him with a gesture. "We must see more of one another," he continued. "I am arranging a grand hunt, and I must have you as my guest of honor. There will be but a few of us, a most select party; and I can assure you of good sport. When all the arrangements are completed, I will let you know the day of the hunt; and now goodbye and good luck to you!"

"I care nothing about him or his grand hunt," said Tarzan as he and Gemnon continued on toward the home of Doria.

"Perhaps it would be well to accept," advised Gemnon. "That fellow and his friends will bear watching, and if you are with them occasionally you can watch them that much better."

Tarzan shrugged. "If I am still here, I shall go with him if you think best."

"If you are still here!" exclaimed Gemnon. "You certainly are not expecting to get away from Cathne, are you?"

"Why, certainly," replied Tarzan. "I may go any day, or night; there is nothing to hold me here, and I have given no promise that I would not escape when I wished."

Gemnon smiled a wry smile that Tarzan did not see in the semi-darkness of the ill-lit avenue through which they were passing. "That will make it extremely interesting for me," he remarked.

"Why?" demanded the ape-man.

"Nemone turned you over into my keeping. If you escape while I am responsible for you she will have me destroyed."

A frown knit the brows of the lord of the jungle. "I did not know that," he said; "but you need not worry; I shall not go until you have been relieved of responsibility." A sudden smile lighted his countenance. "I think I shall ask Nemone to give me over into the keeping of Erot or Xerstle."

Gemnon chuckled. "What a story that would make!" he cried.

An occasional torch only partially dispelled the gloom beneath the overhanging trees that bordered the avenue that led toward the palace of Thudos. At the intersection of a narrow alleyway, beneath the branches of a wide-spreading oak a dark figure lurked in the shadows as Tarzan and Gemnon approached. The keen eyes of the ape-man saw and recognized it as the figure of a man before they came close enough to be in danger; and Tarzan was ready even though he had no suspicion that the man's presence there was in any way concerned with him, for it is the business of the jungle bred to be always ready, whether danger threatens or not.

Just as the two came opposite the figure, Tarzan heard his name whispered in a hoarse voice. He stopped. "Beware of Erot!" whispered the voice. "Tonight!" Then the figure wheeled and lumbered into the denser shadows of the narrow alleyway; but in the glimpse that Tarzan got of it there was a familiar roll to the great body, just as there had been a suggestion of familiarity in the voice.

"Now who do you suppose that is?" demanded Gemnon. "Come on! We'll capture him and find out," and he started as though to pursue the stranger down the alley.

Tarzan laid a restraining hand upon his shoulder. "No," he said; "it was some one who has tried to befriend me. If he wishes to conceal his identity, it is not for me to reveal it."

"You are right," assented Gemnon.

"And I think I would have learned no more by pursuing him than I already know. I recognized him by his voice and his gait, and then, as he turned to leave, a movement in the air brought his scent spoor to my nostrils. I think I would recognize that a mile away, for it is very strong; it always is in powerful men and beasts."

"Why was he afraid of you?" asked Gemnon.

"He was not afraid of me; he was afraid of you because you are a noble."

"He need not have been, if he is a friend of yours. I would not have betrayed him."

"I know that, but he could not. You are a noble, and so you might be a friend of Erot. I do not mind telling you who it was, because I know you would not use the knowledge to harm him; but you will be surprised; I surely was. It was Phobeg."

"No! Why should he befriend the man who defeated and humiliated him, and almost killed him?"

"Because he did *not* kill him. Phobeg is a simple-minded fellow, but he is the type that would not be devoid of gratitude. He is the sort that would bestow doglike devotion upon one who was more powerful than he, for he worships physical prowess."

At the palace of Thudos the two men were ushered into a magnificent apartment by a slave after the guard at the entrance had recognized Gemnon and permitted them to pass. In the soft light of a dozen cressets they awaited

the coming of the daughter of the house to whom the
slave had carried Gemnon's ring to evidence the identity
of her caller. The richness of the furnishings of the room
were scarcely less magnificent than those Tarzan had seen
in the palace of Nemone; and again, here, were the trophies of the chase prominent among the decorations upon
the walls.

A human head, surmounted by a golden helmet, frowned
down from sightless eyes from a place of honor above
the main entrance. Though shrunken and withered in death
there was still strength and majesty in its appearance; and
Tarzan gazed for some moments at it, intrigued by the
thought of all that had passed within that dry and ghastly
skull before it found its way to grace the trophies upon
the palace walls of the noble Thudos. What fierce or kindly
thoughts, what hates, what loves, what rages had been born
and lived and died behind that parchment forehead? What
tales those dried and shrivelled lips might tell could the
hot blood of the fighting man give them life once more!

"A splendid trophy," commented Gemnon, attracted by
his companion's evident interest in the head. "It is the
most valuable trophy in Cathne; there is no other to equal
it, and there may never be another. That head belonged to
a king of Athne. Thudos took it himself in battle as a
young man."

"I rather like the idea," said Tarzan thoughtfully. "In
the world from which I come men fill their trophy rooms
with the heads of creatures who are not their enemies,
who would be their friends if man would let them. Your
most valued trophies are the heads of your enemies who
have had an equal opportunity to take your head. Yes, it
is a splendid idea!"

The light fall of soft sandals upon stone announced the
coming of their hostess, and both men turned toward the
doorway leading into a small open garden from which she
was coming. Tarzan saw a girl of exquisite beauty; but
whether she were more beautiful than Nemone he could
not say, there are so many things that enter into the making
of a beautiful countenance; yet he acknowledged to himself that Thudos was wise in keeping her hidden from the
Queen.

She greeted Gemnon with the sweet familiarity of an

old friend, and when Tarzan was presented her manner was cordial and unaffected, yet always the fact that she was the daughter of Thudos seemed a part of her.

"I saw you in the stadium," she said, and then, with a laugh, "I lost many drachmas because of you."

"I am sorry," said Tarzan. "Perhaps had I known that you were betting on Phobeg I should have let him kill me."

"That is an idea," exclaimed Doria, laughing. "If you fight in the stadium again I shall tell you beforehand which man I am placing my money on, and then I shall be sure to win."

"I see that I must make you like me so well that you will not want to bet on my opponent."

"From what I have seen of him," interjected Gemnon, "I think Tarzan will always be a safe bet—in an arena."

"What do you mean?" demanded the girl. "There is the suggestion of another significance in your words."

"I am afraid my friend will not be so safe in a boudoir," laughed the young noble.

"We have already heard that he has been more than successful," said Doria with just the faintest note of something that might have been disgust.

"Do not judge him too harshly," pleaded Gemnon; "he is still doing his best to get himself destroyed."

"That should not be difficult in the palace of Nemone, though we have already heard startling tales of his refusal to kneel before the Queen. One who has survived that may not have as much to fear as we have imagined," returned Doria.

"Your Queen understands why I do not kneel," explained Tarzan. "It is through no disrespect nor boorish bravado, but because of the habits of a lifetime and the exigencies of my existence. Had I not been commanded to kneel, I might have knelt. I am afraid that I cannot explain the psychology of my position so that another may understand it; but it is plain to me that I must not bow to any authority against my will, unless I am compelled to do so by force."

The three had spent the evening in pleasant conversation, and Gemnon and Tarzan were about to leave, when a middle-aged man entered the room. It was Thudos, the father of Doria. He greeted Gemnon cordially and seemed pleased to meet Tarzan whom he immediately commenced to question relative to the world outside the valleys of Onthar and Thenar.

Thudos was a strikingly handsome man, with strong features, an athletic build, and eyes that were serious and stern that yet had wrinkles at their corners that betokened much laughter. His was a face that one might trust, for integrity, loyalty, and courage had left their imprints plainly upon it, at least for eyes as observant as those of the lord of the jungle.

When the two guests rose to leave again, Thudos seemed satisfied with his appraisal of the stranger. "I am glad that Gemnon brought you," he said. "The very fact that he did convinces me that he has confidence in your friendship and loyalty, for, as you may already know, the position of my house at the court of Nemone is such that we receive only assured friends within our walls."

"I understand," replied the ape-man. He made no other reply, but both Thudos and Doria felt that here was a man who might be trusted.

As the two men entered the avenue in front of the palace of their host, a figure slunk into the shadow of a tree a few paces from them; and neither saw it. Then they walked leisurely toward their apartments in the palace, discussing the noble Thudos and his matchless daughter.

"I have been curious to ask you," said Tarzan, "how Doria dared come to the stadium when her life is constantly in danger should her beauty become known to the Queen?"

"She is always disguised when she goes abroad," replied Gemnon. "A few touches by an expert hand and hollows appear in her cheeks and beneath her eyes, her brow is wrinkled; and behold! she is no longer the most beautiful woman in the world. Nemone would not give her a second thought if she saw her, but still care is taken to see that Nemone does not see her too closely even then. It is informers we fear the most. Thudos never sells a slave who has seen Doria, and once a new slave enters the palace walls he never leaves them again until long years of service have proved him, and his loyalty is unquestioned.

"It is a monotonous life for Doria, the penalty she pays for beauty; but all that we can do is hope and pray that relief will come some day in the death of Nemone or the elevation of Alextar to the throne."

Valthor was asleep on Tarzan's couch when the ape-man entered his bedroom. He had had little rest since his capture, and, in addition, he was suffering from a slight wound; so Tarzan moved softly that he might not disturb him and made no light in the room, the darkness of which was partially dispelled by the moonlight.

Spreading some skins on the floor against the wall opposite the window, the ape-man lay down and was soon asleep, while in the apartment above him two men crouched in the dark beside the window that was directly above that in Tarzan's bedroom.

For a long time they crouched there in silence. One was a large, powerful man; the other smaller and lighter. Fully an hour passed before either moved other than to change a cramped position for one more comfortable; then the smaller man arose. One end of a long rope was knotted about his body beneath his armpits; in his right hand he carried a slim dagger-sword.

Cautiously and silently he went to the window and looked out, his careful gaze searching the grounds below; then he sat on the sill and swung his legs through the window. The larger man, holding the rope firmly with both hands, braced himself. The smaller turned over on his belly and slid out of the window. Hand over hand, the other lowered him; his head disappeared below the sill.

Very carefully, so as to make no noise, the larger man lowered the smaller until the feet of the latter rested on the sill of Tarzan's bedroom window. Here the man reached in and took hold of the casing; then he jerked twice upon the rope to acquaint his fellow with the fact that he had reached his destination safely and the other let the rope slip through his fingers loosely as the movements of the man below dragged it slowly out.

The smaller man stepped gingerly to the floor inside the room. Without hesitation he moved toward the bed, his weapon raised and ready in his hand. He made no haste; his one purpose for the present appeared to be the achievement of absolute silence. It was evident that he feared to awaken the sleeper. Even when he reached the bed he stood there for a long time searching with his eyes for the right spot to strike that the blow might bring instant death. The assassin knew that Gemnon slept in another bedroom across the living room; what he did not know was that Valthor, the Athnean, lay stretched on the bed beneath his keen weapon.

As the assassin hesitated, Tarzan of the Apes opened his eyes. Though the intruder had made no sound his mere presence in the room had aroused the ape-man; perhaps the effluvium from his body, impinging upon the sensitive nostrils of the sleeping beast-man, carried the same message to the alert brain that sound would have carried.

It is said that a sleeping dog awakened by the touch of a cart wheel reacts so quickly that he can escape harm by leaping aside before the wheel crushes him. I do not believe this; but I am convinced that the so-called lower animals awaken in full and complete possession of all their faculties; not slowly, faculty by faculty, as is the case with man. Thus awoke Tarzan, master of all his powers.

At the instant that he opened his eyes he saw the stranger in the room, saw the dagger raised above the form of the sleeping Valthor, read the whole story in a single glance, and in the same moment arose and leaped upon the unsuspecting murderer who was dragged back from his victim at the very instant that his weapon was descending.

As the two men crashed to the floor, Valthor awoke and sprang from his cot; but by the time he had discovered what was transpiring the would-be assassin lay dead upon the floor, and Tarzan of the Apes stood with one foot upon the body of his kill. For an instant the ape-man hesitated, his face upturned as the weird scream of the victorious bull ape trembled on his lips; but then he shook his head, and only a low growl rumbled upward from the deep chest.

Valthor had heard these growls before and was neither surprised nor shocked. The man in the room above had heard only beasts growl, and the sound made him hesitate and wonder. He had heard, too, the crash of the two bodies as Tarzan had hurled the other to the floor, and while he had not interpreted that correctly it had suggested resistance and put him on his guard. Cautiously he stepped closer to the window and looked out, listening.

In the room below, Tarzan of the Apes seized the corpse

of the man who had come to kill him and hurled it through the window into the grounds beneath. The man above saw and, turning, slunk from the room and vanished among the dark shadows of the palace corridors.

14

The Grand Hunt

WITH the breaking of dawn Tarzan and Valthor arose, for the latter was to set out upon his journey to Athne early. The previous evening a slave had been directed to serve breakfast at daybreak, and the two men now heard him arranging the table in the adjoining room.

"We have met again, and again we part," commented Valthor as he fastened his sandal straps to the ivory guards that encircled his ankles. "I wish that you were going with me to Athne, my friend."

"I would go with you were it not for the fact that Gemnon's life would be forfeited should I leave Cathne while he is responsible for me," replied the ape-man, "but you may rest assured that some day I shall pay you a visit in Athne."

"I never expected to see you alive again after we were separated by the flood," continued Valthor, "and when I recognized you in the lion pit I could not believe my own eyes. Four times at least have you saved my life, Tarzan; and you may be assured of a warm welcome in the house of my father at Athne whenever you come."

"The debt, if you feel that there was one, is wiped out," Tarzan assured him, "since you saved my life last night."

"I saved your life! What are you talking about?" demanded Valthor. "How did I save your life?"

"By sleeping in my bed," explained the lord of the jungle.

Valthor laughed. "A courageous, a heroic act!" he mocked.

"But nevertheless it saved my life," insisted the ape-man

"What saved whose life?" demanded a voice at the door.

"Good morning, Gemnon!" greeted Tarzan. "My compliments and congratulations!"

"Thanks! But what about?" demanded the Cathnean.

"Upon your notable ability as a sound sleeper," explained Tarzan, smiling.

Gemnon shook his head dubiously. "Your words are beyond me. What are you talking about?"

"You slept last night through an attempted assassination, the killing of the culprit, and the disposition of his body. Phobeg's warning was no idle gossip."

"You mean that someone came here last night to kill you?"

"And almost killed Valthor instead," and then Tarzan briefly narrated the events of the attempt upon his life.

"Had you ever seen the man before?" asked Gemnon. "Did you recognize him?"

"I paid little attention to him," admitted Tarzan; "I threw him out of the window; but I do not recall having seen him before."

"Was he a noble?"

"No, he was a common warrior. Perhaps you will recognize him when you see him."

"I shall have to have a look at him and report the matter at once," said Gemnon. "Nemone is going to be furious when she hears this."

"She may have instigated it herself," suggested Tarzan; "she is half mad."

"Hush!" cautioned Gemnon. "It is death even to whisper that thought. No, I do not believe it was Nemone; but were you to accuse Erot, M'duze, or Tomos I could easily agree to that. I must go now, and if I do not return before you leave, Valthor, be assured that I have enjoyed entertaining you. It is unfortunate that we are enemies and that the next time we meet we shall have to endeavor to take one another's head."

"It is unfortunate and foolish," replied Valthor.

"But it is the custom," Gemnon reminded him.

"Then may we never meet, for I could never take pleasure in killing you."

"Here's to it, then," cried Gemnon, raising his hand as

though it held a drinking horn. "May we never meet again!" and with that he turned and left them.

Tarzan and Valthor had but scarcely finished their meal when a noble arrived to tell them that Valthor's escort was ready to depart, and a moment later, with a brief farewell, the Athnean left.

Tarzan's liking for Valthor, combined with his curiosity to see the city of ivory, determined him to visit the valley of Thenar before he returned to his own country; but that is a matter apart, having nothing to do with this story, which has seen the last of the likable young noble of Athne.

By Nemone's command the ape-man's weapons had been returned to him, and he was engaged in inspecting them, looking to the points and feathers of his arrows, his bow-string, and his grass rope, when Gemnon returned. The Cathnean was quite evidently angry and not a little excited. This was one of the few occasions upon which Tarzan had seen his warder other than smiling and affable.

"I have had a bad half hour with the Queen," explained Gemnon. "I was lucky to get away with my life. She is furious over this attempt upon your life and blames me for neglect of duty. What am I to do? Sit on your window sill all night?"

Tarzan laughed. "I am an embarrassment," he said lightly, "and I am sorry; but how can I help it? It was an accident that brought me here; it is perversity that keeps me, the perversity of a spoiled woman."

"You had better not tell her that, nor let another than me hear you say it," Gemnon cautioned him.

"I may tell her," laughed Tarzan; "I am afraid I have never acquired that entirely human accomplishment called diplomacy."

"She has sent me to summon you; and I warn you to exercise a little judgment, even though you have no diplomacy. She is like a raging lion, and whoever arouses her further will be in for a mauling."

"What does she want of me?" demanded Tarzan. "Am I to remain in this house, caged up like a pet dog, to run at the beck of a woman?"

"She is investigating this attempt upon your life and has summoned others to be questioned," Gemnon explained.

Gemnon led the way to a large audience chamber where

the nobles of the court were congregated before a massive throne on which the Queen sat, her beautiful brows contracted in a frown. As Tarzan and Gemnon entered the room, she looked up; but she did not smile. A noble advanced and led the two men to seats near the foot of the throne.

As Tarzan glanced about the faces of those near him, he saw Tomos, and Erot, and Xerstle. Erot was nervous; he fidgeted constantly upon his bench; he played with his fingers and with the hilt of his sword; occasionally he glanced appealingly up at Nemone, but if she recognized that he was there, her expression did not acknowledge it.

"We have been awaiting you," said the Queen as Tarzan took his seat. "It appears that you did not exert yourself to hasten in response to our command."

Tarzan looked up at her with an amused smile. "On the contrary, your majesty, I returned at once with the noble Gemnon," he explained respectfully.

"We have summoned you to tell the story of what happened in your apartment last night that resulted in the killing of a warrior." She then turned to a noble standing at her side and whispered a few words in his ear, whereupon the man quit the room. "You may proceed," she said, turning again to Tarzan.

"There is little to tell," replied the ape-man, rising. "A man came to my room to kill me, but I killed him instead."

"How did he enter your room?" demanded Nemone. "Where was Gemnon? Did he admit the fellow?"

"Of course not," replied Tarzan. "Gemnon was asleep in his own room; the man who would have killed me was lowered from the window of the apartment above mine and entered through my window; there was a long rope tied about his body."

"How did you know he came to kill you? Did he attack you?"

"Valthor, the Athnean, was sleeping in my bed; I was sleeping on the floor. The man did not see me, for the room was dark. He went to the bed where he thought I was sleeping. I awoke as he stood over Valthor, his sword raised in his hand ready to strike. Then I killed him and threw his body out of the window."

"Did you recognize him? Had you ever seen him before?" asked the Queen.

"I did not recognize him."

There was a noise at the entrance to the audience chamber that caused Nemone to glance up. Four slaves bore a stretcher into the room and laid it at the foot of the throne; on it was the corpse of a man.

"Is this the fellow who attempted your life?" demanded Nemone.

"It is," replied Tarzan.

She turned suddenly upon Erot. "Did you ever see this man before?" she demanded.

Erot arose. He was white and trembled a little. "But your majesty, he is only a common warrior," he countered; "I may have seen him often, yet have forgotten him; that would not be strange, I see so many of them."

"And you," the Queen addressed a young noble standing near, "have you ever seen this man before?"

"Often," replied the noble; "he was a member of the palace guard and in my company."

"How long has he been attached to the palace?" demanded Nemone.

"Not a month, your majesty."

"And before that? Do you know anything about his prior service?"

"He was attached to the retinue of a noble, your majesty," replied the young officer hesitantly.

"What noble?" demanded Nemone.

"Erot," replied the witness in a low voice.

The Queen looked long and searchingly at Erot. "You have a short memory," she said presently, an undisguised sneer in her voice, "or perhaps you have so many warriors in your retinue that you cannot recall one who has been out of your service for a month!"

Erot was pale and shaken. He looked long at the face of the dead man before he spoke again. "I do recall him now, your majesty, but he does not look the same. Death has changed him; that is why I did not recognize him immediately."

"You are lying," snapped Nemone. "There are some things about this affair that I do not understand; what part you have had in it, I do not know; but I am sure that you had some part, and I am going to find out what. In the meantime you are banished from the palace; there may be others," she looked meaningly at Tomos, "but I shall find them all out, and when I do it will be the lion pit for the lot!"

Rising, she descended from the throne, and all knelt save Tarzan. As she passed him on her way from the chamber, she paused and looked long and searchingly into his eyes. "Be careful," she whispered; "your life is in danger. I dare not see you for a while, for there is one so desperate that not even I could protect you should you visit my apartments again. Tell Gemnon to quit the palace and take you to his father's house. You will be safer there, but even then far from safe. In a few days I shall have removed the obstacles that stand between us; until then, Tarzan, goodbye!"

The ape-man bowed, and the Queen of Cathne passed on out of the audience chamber. The nobles rose. They drew away from Erot and clustered about Tarzan. In disgust the ape-man drew away. "Come, Gemnon," he said; "there is nothing to keep us here longer."

Xerstle blocked their way as they were leaving the chamber. "Everything is ready for the grand hunt," he exclaimed, rubbing his palms together genially. "I thought this tiresome audience would prevent our starting today, but it is still early. The lions and the quarry are awaiting us at the edge of the forest. Get your weapons and join me in the avenue."

Gemnon hesitated. "Who are hunting with you?" he asked.

"Just you and Tarzan and Pindes," explained Xerstle; "a small and select company that ensures a good hunt."

"We will come," said the ape-man.

As the two returned to their quarters to get their weapons Gemnon appeared worried. "I am not sure that it is wise to go," he said.

"And why not?" inquired Tarzan.

"This may be another trap for you."

The ape-man shrugged. "It is quite possible, but I cannot remain cooped up in hiding. I should like to see what a grand hunt is; I have heard the term so often since I came to Cathne. Who is Pindes? I do not recall him."

"He was an officer of the guard when Erot became the Queen's favorite, but through Erot he was dismissed. He is not a bad fellow but weak and easily influenced; however, he must hate Erot, and so I think you have nothing to fear from him."

"I have nothing to fear from anyone," Tarzan assured him.

"Perhaps you think not, but be on guard."

"I am always on guard; had I not been I should have been dead long ago."

"Your self-complacency may be your undoing," growled Gemnon testily.

Tarzan laughed. "I appreciate both danger and my own limitations, but I cannot let fear rob me of my liberty and the pleasures of life; fear is to be more dreaded than death. You are afraid, Erot is afraid, Nemone is afraid; and you are all unhappy. Were I afraid, I should be unhappy but no safer. I prefer to be simply cautious. And by the way, speaking of caution, Nemone instructed me to tell you to take me from the palace and keep me in your father's house. She says the palace is no safe place for me. I really think that it is M'duze who is after me."

"M'duze and Erot and Tomos," said Gemnon; "there is a triumvirate of greed and malice and duplicity that I should hate to have upon my trail."

At his quarters, Gemnon gave orders that his and Tarzan's belongings be moved to the house of his father while the two men were hunting; then they went to the avenue where they found Xerstle and Pindes awaiting them. The latter was a man of about thirty, rather good looking but with a weak face and eyes that invariably dropped from a direct gaze. He met Tarzan with great cordiality, and as the four men walked along the main avenue of the city toward the eastern gate he was most affable.

"You have never been on a grand hunt?" he asked Tarzan.

"No; I have no idea what the term means," replied the ape-man.

"We shall not tell you then, but shall let you see for yourself; then you will enjoy it the more. Of course you hunt much in your own country, I presume."

"I hunt for food only or for my enemies," replied the ape-man.

"You never hunt for pleasure?" demanded Pindes.

"I take no pleasure in killing."

"Well, you won't have to kill today," Pindes assured him; "the lions will do our killing; and I can promise you that you will enjoy the thrill of the chase, that reaches its highest point in the grand hunt."

Beyond the eastern gate an open, parklike plain stretched for a short distance to the forest. Near the gate four stalwart slaves held two lions in leash, while a fifth man, naked but for a dirty loin cloth, squatted upon the ground a short distance away.

As the four hunters approached the party Xerstle explained to Tarzan that the leashed beasts were his hunting lions, and as the ape-man's observant eyes ran over the five men who were to accompany them on the hunt he recognized the stalwart black seated upon the ground apart as the man he had seen upon the auction block in the market place; then Xerstle approached the fellow and spoke briefly with him, evidently giving him orders. When Xerstle had finished, the native started off at a trot across the plain in the direction of the forest. Everyone watched his progress.

"Why is he running ahead?" asked Tarzan. "He will frighten away the quarry."

Pindes laughed. "He is the quarry."

"You mean——" demanded Tarzan with a scowl.

"That this is a grand hunt," cried Xerstle, "where we hunt man, the grandest quarry."

The ape-man's eyes narrowed. "I see," he said; "you are cannibals; you eat the flesh of men."

Gemnon turned away to hide a smile.

"No!" shouted Pindes and Xerstle in unison. "Of course not."

"Then why do you hunt him, if not to eat him?"

"For pleasure," explained Xerstle.

"Oh, yes; I forgot. And what happens if you do not get him? Is he free then?"

"I should say not; not if we can capture him again," cried Xerstle. "Slaves cost too much money to be lightly thrown away like that."

"Tell me more of the grand hunt," insisted Tarzan. "I think I am going to get much satisfaction from this one."

"I hope so," replied Xerstle. "When the quarry reaches the forest we loose the lions; then the sport commences."

"If the fellow takes to the trees," explained Pindes, "we leash the lions and drive him out with sticks and stones or with our spears; then we give him a little start and loose the lions again. Pretty soon they catch him; and it is the aim of the hunters to be in at the kill, for there is where the real thrills come. Have you ever seen two lions kill a man?"

When the black reached the forest, Xerstle spoke a word of command to the keepers and they unleashed the two great beasts. From their actions it was evident that they were trained to the sport. From the moment the native had started out toward the forest the lions had strained and tugged upon their leashes, so that it was only by the use of their spears that the keepers restrained the beasts from dragging them across the plain; and when they were at last set free they bounded away in pursuit of the unfortunate creature who had been chosen to give Xerstle and his guests a few hours of entertainment.

Halfway to the forest the lions settled down to a much slower gait, and the hunters commenced gradually to overhaul them. Xerstle and Pindes appeared excited, far more excited than the circumstances of the hunt warranted; Gemnon was silent and thoughtful; Tarzan was disgusted and bored. But before they reached the forest his interest was aroused, for a plan had occurred to him whereby he might derive some pleasure from the day's sport.

The wood, which the hunters presently entered a short distance behind the lions, was of extraordinary beauty; the trees were very old and gave evidence of having received the intelligent care of man, as did the floor of the forest. There was little or no deadwood in the trees and only occasional clumps of underbrush upon the ground between them. As far as Tarzan could see among the boles of the trees the aspect was that of a well-kept park rather than of a natural wood, and in answer to a comment he made upon this fact Gemnon explained that for ages his people had given regular attention to the conservation of this forest from the city of gold to the Pass of the Warriors.

Heavy lianas swung in graceful loops from tree to tree; higher up toward the sunlight Tarzan caught glimpses of brilliant tropical blooms; there were monkeys in the trees and gaudy, screaming birds. The scene filled the ape-man with such a longing for the freedom that was his life that, for the moment, he almost forgot that Gemnon's life hinged upon his abandoning all thought of escape while the young noble was responsible to the Queen for his safekeeping.

Once within the forest Tarzan dropped gradually to the rear of the party, and then, when none was looking, swung to the branches of a tree. Plain to his nostrils had been the scent spoor of the quarry from the beginning of the chase, and now the ape-man knew, possibly even better than the lions, the direction of the hopeless flight of the doomed black.

Swinging through the trees in a slight detour that carried him around and beyond the hunters without revealing his desertion to them, Tarzan sped through the middle terraces of the forest as only the lord of the jungle can.

Stronger and stronger in his nostrils waxed the scent of the quarry; behind him came the lions and the hunters; and he knew that he must act quickly, for they were no great distance in his rear. A grim smile lighted his grey eyes as he considered the *dénouement* of the project he had undertaken.

Presently he saw the black running through the forest just ahead of him. The fellow was moving at a dogged trot, casting an occasional glance behind him. He was a splendidly muscled Galla, a perfect type of primitive manhood, who seemed bent upon giving the best account of himself that he might against the hopeless odds that must eventually win the game in which his life was the stake. There was neither fear nor panic in his flight, merely inflexible determination to surrender to the inevitable only as a last resort.

Tarzan was directly above the man now, and he spoke to him in the language of his people. "Take to the trees," he called down.

The native looked up, but he did not stop. "Who are you?" he demanded.

"An enemy of your master, who would help you escape," replied the ape-man.

"There is no escape; if I take to the trees they will stone me down."

"They will not find you; I will see to that."

"Why should you help me?" demanded the native, but he stopped now and looked up again, searching for the man whose voice came down to him in a tongue that gave him confidence in the speaker.

"I have told you that I am an enemy of your master."

Now the black saw the bronzed figure of the giant above

him. "You are a white man!" he exclaimed. "You are trying to trick me. Why should a white man help me?"

"Hurry!" admonished Tarzan, "or it will be too late, and no one can help you."

For just an instant longer the African hesitated; then he leaped for a low-hanging branch and swung himself up into the tree as Tarzan came down to meet him.

"They will come soon and stone us both down," he said. There was no hope in his voice nor any fear, only dumb apathy.

15

The Plot that Failed

THROUGH the trees toward the east the ape-man carried the Galla slave who was to have been the victim of Xerstle's day of sport. At first the man had demurred; but as the growling of the hunting lions had increased in volume, denoting their close approach, he had resigned himself to what he may have considered the lesser of two evils.

Swiftly, the giant of the jungle bore the Galla toward the east where, beyond the forest, loomed the mountains that hemmed Onthar upon that side. For a mile he carried him through the trees and then swung lightly to the ground.

"If the lions ever pick up your trail now," he said, "it will not be until long after you have reached the mountains and safety. But do not delay—go now."

The native fell upon his knees and took the hand of his savior in his own. "I am Hafim," he said. "If I could serve you, I would die for you. Who are you?"

"I am Tarzan of the Apes. Now go your way and lose no time."

"One more favor," begged the black.

"What?"

"I have a brother. He, too, was captured by these people when they captured me. He is a slave in the gold mines south of Cathne. His name is Niaka. If you should ever go to the gold mines, tell him that Hafim has escaped. It will make him happier, and perhaps then he will try to escape."

"I shall tell him. Now go."

Silently the African disappeared among the boles of the

forest trees, and Tarzan sprang again into the branches and swung rapidly back in the direction of the hunters. When he reached them, dropping to the ground and approaching them from behind, they were clustered near the spot at which Hafim had taken to the trees.

"Where have you been?" asked Xerstle. "We thought that you had become lost."

"I dropped behind," replied the ape-man; "but where is your quarry? I thought that you would have had him by this time."

"We cannot understand it," admitted Xerstle. "It is evident that he climbed this tree, because the lions followed him to this very spot, where they stood looking up into the tree; but they did not growl as though they saw the man. Then we leashed them again and sent one of the keepers into the tree, but he saw no sign of the quarry."

"It is a mystery!" exclaimed Pindes.

"It is indeed," agreed Tarzan; "at least for those who do not know the secret."

"Who does know the secret?" demanded Xerstle.

"The black slave who has escaped you must know, if no other."

"He has not escaped me," snapped Xerstle. "He has but prolonged the hunt and increased its interest."

"It would add to the excitement of the day to lay some bets on that," said the ape-man. "I do not believe that your lions can again pick up the trail in time to bring down the quarry before dark."

"A thousand drachmas that they do!" cried Xerstle.

"Being a stranger who came naked into your country, I have no thousand drachmas," said Tarzan; "but perhaps Gemnon will cover your bet." He turned his face away from Xerstle and Pindes and, looking at Gemnon, slowly closed one eye.

"Done!" exclaimed Gemnon to Xerstle.

"I only demand the right to conduct the hunt in my own way," said the latter.

"Of course," agreed Gemnon, and Xerstle turned his face toward Pindes and slowly closed one eye.

"We shall separate, then," explained Xerstle, "and as you and Tarzan are betting against me, one of you must accompany me and the other go with Pindes so that all may be sure that the hunt is prosecuted with fairness and determination."

"Agreed," said Tarzan.

"But I am responsible to the Queen for the safe return of Tarzan," demurred Gemnon; "I do not like to have him out of my sight even for a short time."

"I promise that I shall not try to escape," the ape-man assured him.

"It was not that alone of which I was thinking," explained Gemnon.

"And I can assure you that I can take care of myself, if you feel fears for my safety," added Tarzan.

"Come, let us go," urged Xerstle. "I shall hunt with Gemnon and Pindes with Tarzan. We shall take one lion, they the other."

Reluctantly Gemnon assented to the arrangement, and presently the two parties separated, Xerstle and Gemnon going toward the northwest while Pindes and Tarzan took an easterly direction. The latter had proceeded but a short distance, the lion still upon its leash, when Pindes suggested that they separate, spreading out through the forest, and thus combing it more carefully.

"You go straight east," he said to Tarzan, "the keepers and the lion will go northeast, and I will go north. If any comes upon the trail he may shout to attract the others to his position. If we have not located the quarry in an hour let us all converge toward the mountains at the eastern side of the forest."

The ape-man nodded and started off in the direction assigned him, soon disappearing among the trees; but neither Pindes nor the keepers moved from where he had left them, the keepers held by a whispered word from Pindes. The leashed lion looked after the departing ape-man, and Pindes smiled. The keepers looked at him questioningly.

"Such sad accidents have happened many times before," said Pindes.

Tarzan moved steadily toward the east. He knew that he would not find the Negro and so he did not look for him. The forest interested him but not to the exclusion of all else; his keen faculties were always upon the alert. Presently he heard a noise behind him and glancing back was not surprised by what he saw. A lion was stalking him, a lion wearing the harness of a hunting lion of Cathne. It was one of Xerstle's lions; it was the same lion that had accompanied Pindes and Tarzan.

Instantly the ape-man guessed the truth, and a grim light glinted in his eyes; it was no light of anger, but there was disgust in it and the shadowy suggestion of a savage smile. The lion, realizing that its quarry had discovered it, began to roar. In the distance Pindes heard and smiled.

"Let us go now," he said to the keepers; "we must not find the remains too quickly; that might not look well." The three men moved slowly off toward the north.

From a distance Gemnon and Xerstle heard the roar of the hunting lion. "They have picked up the trail," said Gemnon, halting; "we had best join them."

"Not yet," demurred Xerstle. "It may be a false trail. The animal with them is not so good a hunter as ours; he is not so well trained. We will wait until we hear the hunters call." But Gemnon was troubled.

Tarzan stood waiting the coming of the lion. He could have taken to the trees and escaped, but a spirit of bravado prompted him to remain. He hated treachery, and exposing it gave him pleasure. He carried a Cathnean spear and his own hunting knife; his bow and arrows he had left behind.

The lion came nearer; it seemed vaguely disturbed. Perhaps it did not understand why the quarry stood and faced it instead of running away. Its tail twitched; its head was flattened; slowly it came on again, its wicked eyes gleaming angrily.

Tarzan waited. In his right hand was the sturdy Cathnean spear, in his left the hunting knife of the father he had never known. He measured the distance with a trained eye as the lion started its swift, level charge; then, when it was coming at full speed, his spear hand flew back and he launched the heavy weapon.

Deep beneath the left shoulder it drove, deep into the savage heart; but it checked the beast's charge for but an instant. Infuriated now, the carnivore rose upon its hind legs above the ape-man, its great, taloned paws reaching to drag him to the slavering jowls; but Tarzan, swift as Ara, the lightning, stooped and sprang beneath them, sprang to one side and then in again, closing with the lion, leaping upon its back.

With a hideous roar, the animal wheeled and sought to bury its great fangs in the bronzed body or reach it with those raking talons. It threw itself to right and left as the creature clinging to it drove a steel blade repeatedly into the already torn and bleeding heart.

The vitality and life tenacity of a lion are astounding; but even that mighty frame could not for long withstand the lethal wounds its adversary had inflicted, and presently it slumped to earth and, with a little quiver, died. Then the ape-man leaped to his feet. With one foot upon the carcass of his kill, Tarzan of the Apes raised his face to the leafy canopy of the Cathnean forest and from his great chest rolled the hideous victory cry of the bull ape which has killed.

As the uncanny challenge reverberated down the forest aisles, Pindes and the two keepers looked questioningly at one another and laid their hands upon their sword hilts.

"In the name of Thoos! what was that?" demanded one of the keepers.

"By the name of Thoos! I never heard a sound so horrible before," answered his companion, looking fearfully in the direction from which those weird notes had come.

"Silence!" admonished Pindes. "Do you want the thing to creep upon us unheard because of your jabbering!"

"What was it, master?" asked one of the men in a whisper.

"It may have been the death cry of the stranger," suggested Pindes, voicing the hope that was in his heart.

"It sounded not like a death cry, master," replied the black; "there was a note of strength and elation in it and none of weakness and defeat."

"Silence, fool!" grumbled Pindes.

At a little distance, Gemnon and Xerstle heard, too. "What was that?" demanded the latter.

Gemnon shook his head. "I do not know, but we had better go and find out. I did not like the sound of it."

Xerstle appeared nervous. "It was nothing, perhaps, but the wind in the trees; let us go on with our hunting."

"There is no wind," demurred Gemnon. "I am going to investigate. I am responsible for the safety of the stranger; but, even of more importance than that, I like him."

"Oh, so do I!" exclaimed Xerstle eagerly. "But nothing could have happened to him; Pindes is with him."

"That is precisely what I was thinking," observed Gemnon.

"That nothing could have happened to him?"

"That Pindes is with him!"

Xerstle shot a quick, suspicious look at the other, motioned to the keepers to follow with the leashed lion, and fell in behind Gemnon who had already started back toward the point at which they had separated from their companions.

In the meantime Pindes, unable to curb his curiosity, overcame his fears and started after Tarzan for the purpose of ascertaining what had befallen him as well as tracing the origin of the mysterious cry that had so filled him and his servants with wondering awe. Rather nervously, the two lion keepers followed him through the brooding silence of the forest, all three men keeping a careful lookout ahead and upon every side.

They had not gone far when Pindes, who was in the lead, halted suddenly and pointed straight ahead. "What is that?" he demanded.

The keepers pressed forward. "Mane of Thoos!" cried one, "it is the lion!"

They advanced slowly, watching the lion, looking to right and left. "It is dead!" exclaimed Pindes.

The three men examined the body of the dead beast, turning it over. "It has been stabbed to death," announced one of the keepers.

"The Galla slave had no weapon," said Pindes thoughtfully.

"The stranger carried a knife," a keeper reminded him.

"Whoever killed the lion must have fought it hand-to-hand," reflected Pindes aloud.

"Then he must be lying nearby dead or wounded, master."

"Search for him!" directed Pindes.

"He could have killed Phobeg with his bare hands that day that he threw him into the audience at the stadium," a keeper reminded the noble. "He carried him around as though Phobeg were a babe. He is very strong."

"What has that to do with the matter?" demanded Pindes irritably.

"I do not know, master; I was only thinking."

"I did not tell you to think," snapped Pindes; "I told you to hunt for the man that killed the lion; he must be dying or dead nearby."

While they hunted, Xerstle and Gemnon were drawing nearer. The latter was much concerned about the welfare of his charge. He trusted neither Xerstle nor Pindes, and now he commenced to suspect that he and Tarzan had been deliberately separated for sinister purposes. He was walking a little behind Xerstle at the time; the keepers, with the lion, were just ahead of them. He felt a hand upon his shoulder and wheeled about; there stood Tarzan, a smile upon his lips.

"Where did you drop from?" demanded Gemnon.

"We separated to search for the Galla, Pindes and I," explained the ape-man as Xerstle turned at the sound of Gemnon's voice and discovered him.

"Did you hear that terrible scream a while ago?" demanded Xerstle. "We thought it possible that one of you was hurt, and we were hurrying to investigate."

"Did some one scream?" inquired Tarzan innocently. "Perhaps it was Pindes, for I am not hurt."

Shortly after Tarzan had rejoined them Xerstle and Gemnon came upon Pindes and his two lion keepers searching the underbrush and the surrounding forest. As his eyes fell upon Tarzan, Pindes' eyes went wide in astonishment, and he paled a little.

"What has happened?" demanded Xerstle. "What are you looking for? Where is your lion?"

"He is dead," explained Pindes. "Some one or something stabbed him to death." He did not look at Tarzan; he feared to do so. "We have been looking for the man who did it, thinking that he must have been badly mauled and, doubtless, killed."

"Have you found him?" asked Tarzan.

"No."

"Shall I help you search for him? Suppose you and I, Pindes, go away alone and look for him!" suggested the ape-man.

For a moment Pindes seemed choking as he sought for a

reply. "No!" he exclaimed presently. "It would be useless; we have searched carefully; there is not even a sign of blood to indicate that he was wounded."

"And you found no trace of the quarry?" asked Xerstle.

"None," replied Pindes. "He has escaped, and we might as well return to the city. I have had enough hunting for today."

Xerstle grumbled. It was getting late; he had lost his quarry and one of his lions; but there seemed no reason to continue the hunt, and so he grudgingly acquiesced.

"So this is a grand hunt?" remarked Tarzan meditatively "Perhaps it has not been thrilling; but I have enjoyed it greatly. However, Gemnon appears to be the only one who has profited by it; he has won a thousand drachmas."

Xerstle only grunted and strode on moodily toward the city. When the party separated before the house of Gemnon's father Tarzan stood close to Xerstle and whispered in a low voice. "My compliments to Erot, and may he have better luck next time!"

16

In the Temple of Thoos

As Tarzan sat with Gemnon and the latter's father and mother at dinner that evening a slave entered the room to announce that a messenger had come from the house of Thudos, the father of Doria, with an important communication for Gemnon.

"Fetch him here," directed the young noble, and a moment later a tall Negro was ushered into the apartment.

"Ah, Gemba!" exclaimed Gemnon in a kindly tone, "you have a message for me?"

"Yes, master," replied the slave, "but it is important—and secret."

"You may speak before these others, Gemba," replied Gemnon. "What is it?"

"Doria, the daughter of Thudos, my master, has sent me to tell you that by a ruse the noble Erot gained entrance to her father's house and spoke with her today. What he said to her was of no importance; only the fact that he saw her is important."

"The jackal!" exclaimed Gemnon's father.

Gemnon paled. "That is all?" he inquired.

"That is all, master," replied Gemba.

Gemnon took a gold coin from his pocket pouch and handed it to the slave. "Return to your mistress, and tell her that I shall come and speak with her father tomorrow."

After the slave had withdrawn Gemnon looked hopelessly at his father. "What can I do?" he asked. "What can Thudos do? What can anyone do? We are helpless."

"Perhaps I can do something," suggested Tarzan. "For the moment I seem to hold the confidence of your Queen; when I see her I shall question her, and if it is necessary I shall intercede in your behalf."

A new hope sprang to Gemnon's eyes. "If you will!" he cried. "She will listen to you. I believe that you alone might save Doria; but remember that the Queen must not see her, for should she, nothing can save her—she will be either disfigured or killed."

Early the next morning a messenger from the palace brought a command to Tarzan to visit the Queen at noon, with instructions to Gemnon to accompany Tarzan with a strong guard as she feared treachery on the part of Tarzan's enemies.

"They must be powerful enemies that dare attempt to thwart the wishes of Nemone," commented Gemnon's father.

"There is only one in all Cathne who dares do that," replied Gemnon.

The older man nodded. "The old she-devil! Would but that Thoos destroyed her! How shameful it is that Cathne should be ruled by a slave woman!"

"I have seen Nemone look at her as though she wished to kill her," said Tarzan.

"Yes, but she will never dare," prophesied Gemnon's father. "Between the old witch and Tomos a threat of some sort is held over the Queen's head so that she dares not destroy either one of them, yet I am sure she hates them both; and it is seldom that she permits one to live whom she hates."

"It is thought that they hold the secret of her birth, a secret that would destroy her if it were announced to the people," explained Gemnon; "but come, we have the morning to ourselves; I shall not visit Thudos until after you have talked with Nemone; what shall we do in the meantime?"

"I should like to visit the mines of Cathne," replied Tarzan; "shall we have time?"

"Yes, we shall," replied Gemnon; "the Mine of the Rising Sun is not far; and as there is little to see after you get there, the trip will not take long."

On the road from Cathne to the nearer mine, Gemnon pointed out the breeding plant where the war and hunting lions of Cathne are bred; but they did not stop to visit the place, and presently they were winding up the short mountain road to the Gold Mine of the Rising Sun.

As Gemnon had warned him, there was little of interest for Tarzan to see. The workings were open, the mother lode lying practically upon the surface of the ground; and so rich was it that only a few slaves working with crude picks and bars were needed to supply the coffers of Cathne with vast quantities of the precious metal. But it was not the mines nor gold that had caused Tarzan to wish to visit the diggings. He had promised Hafim that he would carry a message to his brother, Niaka; and it was for this purpose that he had suggested the visit.

As he moved about among the slaves, ostensibly inspecting the lode, he finally succeeded in separating himself sufficiently from Gemnon and the warriors who guarded the workers to permit him to speak unnoticed to one of the slaves.

"Which is Niaka?" he asked in Galla, lowering his voice to a whisper.

The black looked up in surprise, but at a warning gesture from Tarzan bent his head again and answered in a whisper, "Niaka is the big man at my right. He is headman; you see that he does not work."

Tarzan moved then in the direction of Niaka, and when he was close stopped beside him and leaned as though inspecting the lode that was uncovered at his feet. "Listen," he whispered. "I bring you a message, but let no one know that I am talking to you. It is from your brother, Hafim. He has escaped."

"How?" whispered Niaka.

Briefly, Tarzan explained.

"It was you, then, who saved him?"

The ape-man nodded.

"I am only a poor slave," said Niaka, "and you are a powerful noble, no doubt; so I can never repay you. But should you ever need any service that Niaka can render, you have but to command; with my life I would serve you. In that little hut below the diggings I live with my woman; because I am headman I am trusted and live thus alone. If you ever want me you will find me there."

"I ask no return for what I did," replied Tarzan, "but I

shall remember where you live; one never knows what the future holds."

He moved away then and joined Gemnon; and presently the two turned back toward the city, while in the palace of the Queen Tomos entered the apartment of Nemone and knelt.

"What now?" she demanded. "Is the affair so urgent that I must be interrupted at my toilet?"

"It is, majesty," replied the councillor, "and I beg that you send your slaves away. What I have to say is for your ears alone."

There were four Negro girls working on Nemone's nails, one at each foot and one at each hand, and a white girl arranging her hair. To the last the Queen spoke, "Take the slaves away, Maluma, and send them to their quarters; you may wait in the adjoining room."

Then she turned to the councillor, who had arisen. "Well, what is it?"

"Your majesty has long had reason to suspect the loyalty of Thudos," Tomos reminded her, "and in the interest of your majesty's welfare and the safety of the throne, I am constantly watchful of the activities of this powerful enemy. Spurred on by love and loyalty, the noble Erot has been my most faithful agent and ally; and it is really to him that we owe the information that I bring you."

Nemone tapped her sandalled foot impatiently upon the mosaic floor. "Have done with the self-serving preamble, and tell me what you have to tell me," she snapped, for she did not like Tomos and made no effort to hide her feelings.

"Briefly, then, it is this; Gemnon conspires also with Thudos, hoping, doubtless, that his reward will be the beautiful daughter of his chief."

"That hollow-checked strumpet!" exclaimed Nemone. "Who said she was beautiful?"

"Erot tells me that Gemnon and Thudos believe her the most beautiful woman in the world," replied Tomos.

"Impossible! Did Erot see her?"

"Yes, majesty, he saw her."

"What does Erot say?" demanded the Queen.

"That she is indeed beautiful," replied the councillor. "There are others who think so too," he added.

"What others?"

"One who has been drawn into the conspiracy with Gemnon and Thudos by the beauty of Doria, the daughter of Thudos."

"Whom do you mean? Speak out! I know you have something unpleasant in your mind that you are suffering to tell me, hoping that it will make me unhappy."

"Oh, majesty, you wrong me!" cried Tomos. "My only thoughts are for the happiness of my beloved Queen."

"Your words stink with falseness," sneered Nemone. "But get to the point; I have other matters to occupy my time."

"I but hesitated to name the other for fear of wounding your majesty," said Tomos oilily; "but if you insist, it is the stranger called Tarzan."

Nemone sat up very straight. "What fabric of lies is this you and M'duze are weaving?" she demanded.

"It is no lie, majesty. Tarzan and Gemnon were seen coming from the house of Thudos late at night. Erot had followed them there; he saw them go in; they were there a long while; hiding in the shadows across the avenue, he saw them come out. He says that they were quarrelling over Doria, and he believes that it was Gemnon who sought the life of Tarzan because of jealousy."

Nemone sat straight and stiff upon her couch; her face was pale and tense with fury. "Some one shall die for this," she said in a low voice. "Go!"

Tomos backed from the room. He was elated until he had time to reflect more fully upon her words; then he reflected that Nemone had not stated explicitly who should die. He had assumed that she meant Tarzan, because it was Tarzan whom he wished to die; but it presently occurred to him that she might have meant another, and he was less elated.

It was almost noon when Tarzan and Gemnon returned to the city, and time for the latter to conduct Tarzan to his audience with Nemone. With a guard of warriors they went to the palace, where the ape-man was immediately admitted alone into the presence of the Queen.

"Where have you been?" she demanded.

Tarzan looked at her in surprise; then he smiled. "I visited the Mine of the Rising Sun."

"Where were you last night?"

"At the house of Gemnon," he replied.

"You were with Doria!" accused Nemone.

"No," said the ape-man; "that was the night before."

He had been surprised by the accusation and the knowledge that it connoted, but he did not let her see that he was surprised. He was not thinking of himself but of Doria and Gemnon, seeking a plan whereby he might protect them. It was evident that some enemy had turned informer and that Nemone already knew of the visit to the house of Thudos; therefore he felt that it would but have aroused the Queen's suspicions to have denied it; to admit it freely, to show that he sought to conceal nothing, would allay them. As a matter of fact Tarzan's frank and ready reply left Nemone rather flat.

"Why did you go to the house of Thudos?" she asked, but this time her tone was not accusing.

"You see, Gemnon does not dare to leave me alone for fear that I shall escape or that something may befall me; and so he is forced to take me wherever he goes. It is rather hard on him, Nemone, and I have been intending to ask you to make some one else responsible for me for at least a part of the time."

"We will speak of that later," replied the Queen. "Why does Gemnon got to the house of Thudos?" Nemone's eyes narrowed suspiciously.

The ape-man smiled. "What a foolish question for a woman to ask!" he exclaimed. "Gemnon is in love with Doria. I thought all Cathne knew that; he certainly takes enough pains to tell all his acquaintances."

"You are sure that it is not you who are in love with her?" demanded Nemone.

Tarzan looked at her with disgust he made no effort to conceal. "Do not be a fool, Nemone," he said. "I do not like foolish women."

The jaw of the Queen of Cathne dropped. In all her life no one had ever addressed her in words or tones like these. For a moment they left her speechless, but in that moment of speechlessness there came the sudden realization that the very things that shocked her also relieved her mind of gnawing suspicion and of jealousy—Tarzan did not love Doria. And, too, she was compelled to admit that his indifference to her position or her anger increased her respect for him and made him still more desirable in her eyes. She had never known such a man before; none had ever ruled her. Here was one who might if he wished, but she was troubled by the fear that he did not care enough about her to wish to rule her.

When she spoke again, she had regained her calm. "I was told that you loved her," she explained, "but I did not believe it. Is she very beautiful? I have heard that she is considered the most beautiful woman in Cathne."

"Perhaps Gemnon thinks so," replied Tarzan with a laugh, "but you know what love does to the eyes of youth."

"What do you think of her?" demanded the Queen.

The ape-man shrugged. "She is not bad looking," he said.

"Is she as beautiful as Nemone?" demanded the Queen.

"As the brilliance of a far star is to the brilliance of the sun."

The reply appeared to please Nemone. She arose and came closer to Tarzan. "You think me beautiful?" she asked in soft, insinuating tones.

"You are very beautiful, Nemone," he answered truthfully.

She pressed against him, caressing his shoulder with a smooth, warm palm. "Love me, Tarzan," she whispered, her voice husky with emotion.

There was a rattling of chains at the far end of the room, followed by a terrific roar as Belthar sprang to his feet. Nemone shrank suddenly away from the ape-man; a shudder ran through her body, and an expression, half fright, half anger, suffused her face.

"It is always something," she said irritably, trembling a little. "Belthar is jealous. There is a strange bond linking the life of that beast to my life. I do not know what it is; I wish I did." A light, almost of madness, glittered in her eyes. "I wish I knew! Sometimes I think he is the mate that Thoos intended for me; sometimes I think he is myself in another form; but this I know: When Belthar dies, I die!"

She looked up rather sadly at Tarzan as again her mood changed. "Come, my friend," she said; "we shall go to the temple together and perhaps Thoos may answer the questions that are in the heart of Nemone." She struck a bronze disc that depended from the ceiling, and as the brazen notes reverberated in the room a door opened and a noble bowed low upon the threshold.

"The guard!" commanded the Queen. "We are visiting Thoos in his temple."

The progress to the temple was in the nature of a pageant —marching warriors with pennons streaming from spear tips, nobles resplendent in gorgeous trappings, the Queen in a golden chariot drawn by lions. Tomos walked upon one side of the glittering car, Tarzan upon the other where Erot had previously walked.

The ape-man was as uneasy as a forest lion as he strode between the lines of gaping citizenry. Crowds annoyed and irritated him; formalities irked him; his thoughts were far away in the distant jungle that he loved. He knew that Gemnon was nearby watching him; but whether he were nearby or not, Tarzan would not attempt to escape while this friend was responsible for him. His mind occupied with such thoughts, he spoke to the Queen.

"At the palace," he reminded her, "I spoke to you concerning the matter of relieving Gemnon of the irksome job of watching me."

"Gemnon has acquitted himself well," she replied. "I see no reason for changing."

"Relieve him then occasionally," suggested Tarzan. "Let Erot take his place."

Nemone looked at him in astonishment. "But Erot hates you!" she exclaimed.

"All the more reason that he would watch me carefully," argued Tarzan.

"He would probably kill you."

"He would not dare if he knew that he must pay for my death or escape with his own life," suggested Tarzan.

"You like Gemnon, do you not?" inquired Nemone innocently.

"Very much," the ape-man assured her.

"Then he is the man to watch you, for you would not imperil his life by escaping while he is responsible."

Tarzan smiled inwardly and said no more; it was evident that Nemone was no fool. He would have to devise some other plan of escape that would not jeopardize the safety of his friend.

They were approaching the temple now and his attention was distracted by the approach of a number of priests leading a slave girl in chains. They brought her to the chariot of

Nemone, and while the procession halted the priests chanted in a strange gibberish that Tarzan could not understand. Later he learned that no one understood it, not even the priests; but when he asked why they recited something that they could not understand no one could tell him.

Gemnon thought that once the words had meant something, but they had been repeated mechanically for so many ages that at length the original pronunciation had been lost and the meaning of the words forgotten.

When the chant was completed the priests chained the girl to the rear of the Queen's chariot; and the march was resumed, the priests following behind the girl.

At the entrance to the temple Phobeg was on guard as a girl entered to worship. Recognizing the warrior, she greeted him and paused for a moment's conversation, the royal party having not yet entered the temple square.

"I have not seen you to talk with for a long time, Phobeg," she said. "I am glad that you are back again on the temple guard."

"Thanks to the stranger called Tarzan I am alive and here," replied Phobeg.

"I should think that you would hate him," exclaimed the girl.

"Not I," cried Phobeg. "I know a better man when I see one. I admire him. And did he not grant me my life when the crowd screamed for my death?"

"That is true," admitted the girl. "And now *he* needs a friend."

"What do you mean, Maluma?" demanded the warrior.

"I was in an adjoining room when Tomos visited the Queen this morning," explained the girl, "and I overheard him tell her that Thudos and Gemnon and Tarzan were conspiring against her and that Tarzan loved Doria, the daughter of Thudos."

"How did Tomos know these things?" asked Phobeg. "Did he offer proof?"

"He said that Erot had watched and had seen Gemnon and Tarzan visit the house of Thudos," explained Maluma. "He also told her that Erot had seen Doria and had reported that she was very beautiful."

Phobeg whistled. "That will be the end of the daughter of Thudos," he said.

"It will be the end of the stranger, too," phophesied Maluma; "and I am sorry, for I like him. He is not like the jackal, Erot, whom everyone hates."

"Here comes the Queen!" exclaimed Phobeg as the head of the procession debouched into the temple square. "Run along now and get a good place, for there will be something to see today; there always is when the Queen comes to worship god."

Before the temple, Nemone alighted from her chariot and walked up the broad stairway to the ornate entrance. Behind her were the priests with the slave girl, a frightened, wide-eyed girl with tears upon her cheeks. Following them came the nobles of the court, the warriors of the guard remaining in the temple square before the entrance.

The temple was a large three-storied building with a great central dome about the interior of which ran galleries at the second and third stories. The interior of the dome was of gold as were the pillars that supported the galleries, while the walls of the building were embellished with colorful mosaics. Directly opposite the main entrance, on a level with a raised dais, a great cage was built into a niche, and on either side of the cage was an altar supporting a lion carved from solid gold. Before the dais was a stone railing inside of which was a throne and a row of stone benches facing the cage in the niche.

Nemone advanced and seated herself upon the throne, while the nobles took their places upon the benches. No one paid any attention to Tarzan; so he remained outside the railing, a mildly interested spectator.

He had noticed a change come over Nemone the instant that she had entered the temple. She had shown signs of extreme nervousness, the expression of her face had changed; it was tense and eager; there was a light in her eyes that was like the mad light he had seen there occasionally before, yet different—the light of religious fanaticism.

Tarzan saw the priests lead the girl up onto the dais and then, beyond them, he saw something rise up in the cage. It was an old and mangy lion. The high priest began a meaningless, singsong chant, in which the others joined occasionally as though making responses. Nemone leaned forward eagerly; her eyes were fastened upon the old lion. Her breasts rose and fell to her excited breathing.

Suddenly the chanting ceased and the Queen arose. "O Thoos!" she cried, her hands outstretched toward the mangy old carnivore. "Nemone brings you greetings and an offering. Receive them from Nemone and bless her. Give her life and health and happiness; most of all Nemone prays for happiness. Preserve her friends and destroy her enemies. And, O Thoos, give her the one thing that she most desires— love, the love of the one man in all the world that Nemone has ever loved!" And the lion glared at her through the bars.

She spoke as though in a trance, as though oblivious to all else around her save the god to which she prayed. There were pathos and tragedy in her voice, and a great pity rose in the breast of the ape-man for this poor Queen who had never known love and who never might because of the warped brain that mistook passion for affection and lust for love.

As she sat down weakly upon her golden throne, the priests led the slave girl away through a doorway at one side of the cage; and, as she passed, the lion leaped for her, striking heavily against the bars that restrained him. His growls rolled through the temple, filling the chamber with thunderous sound, echoing and reëchoing from the golden dome.

Nemone sat, silent and rigid, upon her throne staring straight ahead at the lion in the cage; the priests and many of the nobles were reciting prayers in monotones. It was evident to Tarzan that they were praying to the lion, for every eye was upon the repulsive beast; and some of the questions that had puzzled him when he had first come to Cathne were answered. He understood now the strange oaths of Phobeg and his statement that he had stepped upon the tail of god.

Suddenly a beam of light shone down directly into the cage from above, flooding the beast-god with its golden rays. The lion, which had been pacing restlessly to and fro, stopped and looked up, his jaws parted, saliva dripping from his jowls. The audience burst in unison into a singsong chant. Tarzan, half guessing what was about to occur, arose from the rail upon which he had been sitting, and started forward.

But whatever his intention may have been, he was too late to prevent the tragedy that followed instantly. Even as he arose the body of the slave girl dropped from above into the clutches of the waiting lion. A single piercing scream mingled with the horrid roars of the man-eater and then died as its author died.

Tarzan turned away in disgust and anger and walked from the temple out into the fresh air and the sunlight, and as he did so a warrior at the entrance hailed him by name in a whisper. There was a cautionary warning in the voice that prompted the ape-man to give no apparent sign of having heard as he turned his eyes casually in the direction from which the words had come, nor did he betray his interest when he discovered that it was Phobeg who had addressed him.

Turning slowly, so that his back was toward the warrior, Tarzan looked back into the temple as though expecting the return of the royal party; then he backed to the side of the entrance as one might who waits and stood so close to Phobeg that the latter might have touched him by moving his spear hand a couple of inches; but neither gave any sign of being aware of the identity or presence of the other.

In a low whisper, through lips that scarcely moved, Phobeg spoke. "I must speak to you! Come to the rear of the temple two hours after the sun has set. Do not answer, but if you hear and will come, turn your head to the right."

As Tarzan gave the assenting signal the royal party commenced to file from the temple, and he fell in behind Nemone. The Queen was quiet and moody, as she always was after the sight of torture and blood at the temple had aroused her to religious frenzy; the reaction left her weak and indifferent. At the palace, she dismissed her following, including Tarzan, and withdrew to the seclusion of her apartments.

17

The Secret of the Temple

AFTER the royal party left the temple Maluma came out and paused again to gossip with Phobeg. For some time they talked before she bid him goodbye and started back toward the palace. They spoke of many things —of the man in the secret prison behind a heavy golden door beneath the temple floor, of Erot and Tomos, of Nemone and Tarzan, of Gemnon and Doria, and of themselves. Being human, they talked mostly of themselves. It was late when Maluma returned to the palace. It was already the evening meal hour.

In the home of his father, Gemnon paced the floor of the patio as he awaited the summons to the evening meal. Tarzan half sat, half reclined upon a stone bench. He saw that his friend was worried; and it troubled him, troubled him most perhaps because he knew that there were grave causes for apprehension; and he was not certain that he could avert the disaster that threatened.

Seeking to divert Gemnon's mind from his troubles, Tarzan spoke of the ceremony at the temple, but principally of the temple itself, praising its beauty, commenting upon its magnificence. "It is splendid," he commented; "too splendid for the cruel rites we witnessed there today."

"The girl was only a slave," replied Gemnon, "and god must eat. It is no wrong to make offerings to Thoos; but the temple *does* hide a real wrong. Somewhere within it is hidden Alextar, the brother of Nemone; and while he rots there the corrupt Tomos and the cruel M'duze rule Cathne through the mad Nemone.

"There are many who would have a change and place Alextar on the throne, but they fear the wrath of the terrible triumvirate. So we go on, and nothing is done. Victim after victim succumbs to the malignant jealousy and fear that constantly animate the throne.

"We have little hope today; we shall have no hope if the Queen carries out the plan she is believed to be contemplating and destroys Alextar. There are reasons why it would be to her advantage to do so, the most important being the right of Alextar to proclaim himself king should he ever succeed in reaching the palace.

"If Nemone should die Alextar would become king, and the populace would insist that he take his rightful place. For this reason Tomos and M'duze are anxious to destroy him. It is to Nemone's credit that she has withstood their importunities for all these years, steadfastly refusing to destroy Alextar; but if ever he seriously threatens her power, he is lost; and rumors that have reached her ears that a plot has been perfected to place him on the throne may already have sealed his doom."

During the meal that evening Tarzan considered plans for visiting Phobeg at the temple. He wished to go alone but knew that he would place Gemnon in an embarrassing position should he suggest such a plan, while to permit the noble to accompany him might not only seal Phobeg's lips but jeopardize his safety as well; therefore he decided to go secretly.

Following the stratagem he had adopted, he remained in conversation with Gemnon and his parents until almost two hours after the sun had set; then he excused himself, saying that he was tired, and went to the room that had been assigned him. But he did not tarry there. Instead, he merely crossed the room from the door to the window and stepped out into the patio upon which it faced. Here, as throughout the gardens and avenues of the section of the city occupied by the nobility, grew large, old trees; and a moment later the lord of the jungle was swinging through his native element toward the golden temple of Thoos.

He stopped at last in a tree near the rear of the temple where he saw the huge and familiar figure of Phobeg waiting in the shadows below. Soundlessly, the ape-man dropped to the ground in front of the astonished warrior.

"By the great fangs of Thoos!" ejaculated Phobeg, "but you gave me a start."

"You expected me," was Tarzan's only comment.

"But not from the skies," retorted Phobeg. "However, you are here and it is well; I have much more to tell you than when I asked you to come. I have learned more since."

"I am listening," said Tarzan.

"A girl in the service of the Queen overheard a conversation between Nemone and Tomos," commenced Phobeg. "Tomos accused you and Gemnon and Thudos of conspiring against her. Erot spied upon you and knew of your long visit at the home of Thudos a few nights since; he also managed to enter the house on some pretext the following night and saw Doria, the daughter of Thudos. Tomos told Nemone that Doria was very beautiful and that you were in love with her.

"Nemone is not yet convinced that you love Doria, but to be on the safe side she has ordered Tomos to have the girl abducted and brought to the temple where she will be imprisoned until Nemone decides upon her fate. She may destroy her, or she may be content to have her beauty disfigured.

"But what you must know is this: If you give Nemone the slightest reason to believe that you are conspiring against her or that you are fond of Doria she will have you killed. All that I can do is warn you."

"You warned me once before, did you not?" asked Tarzan, "the night that Gemnon and I went to the house of Thudos."

"Yes, that was I," replied Phobeg.

"Why have you done these things?" asked the ape-man.

"Because I owe my life to you," replied the warrior, "and because I know a man when I see one. If a man can pick Phobeg up and toss him around as though he were a baby, Phobeg is willing to be his slave."

"I can only thank you for what you have told me, Phobeg," said Tarzan. "Now tell me more. If Doria is brought to the temple where will she be imprisoned?"

"That is hard to say. Alextar is kept in rooms beneath the floor of the temple, but there are rooms upon the second and third floors where a prisoner might be safely confined, especially a woman."

"Could you get word to me if she is arrested?"

"I could try," replied Phobeg.

"Good! Is there anything further?"

"No."

"Then I shall return to Gemnon and warn him. Perhaps we shall find a way to pacify Nemone or outwit her."

"Either would be difficult," commented Phobeg, "but goodbye and good luck!"

Tarzan swung into the tree above the warrior's head and disappeared among the shadows of the night, while Phobeg shook his head in wonderment and returned to his quarters in the temple.

The ape-man made his way to his room by the same avenue he had left it and went immediately to the common living room where the family ordinarily congregated for the evenings. Here he found Gemnon's father and mother, but Gemnon was not there.

"You could not sleep?" inquired the mother.

"No," replied the ape-man. "Where is Gemnon?"

"He was summoned to the palace a short time after you went to your room," explained Gemnon's father.

Announcing that he would wait up until the son returned, Tarzan remained in the living room in conversation with the parents. He wondered a little that Gemnon should have been summoned to the palace at such an hour; and the things that Phobeg had told him made him a little apprehensive, but he kept his own council rather than frighten his host and hostess.

Scarcely an hour had passed when they heard a summons at the outer gate, and presently a slave came to announce that a warrior wished to speak to Tarzan upon a matter of urgent necessity.

The ape-man arose. "I will go outside and see him," he said.

"Be careful," cautioned Gemnon's father. "You have bitter enemies who would be glad to see you destroyed."

"I shall be careful," Tarzan assured him as he left the room behind the slave.

At the gate two warriors connected with the house were detaining a huge man whom Tarzan recognized even from a distance as Phobeg. "I must speak with you at once and alone," said the latter.

"This man is all right," Tarzan told the guards. "Let him enter and I will talk with him in the garden."

When they had walked a short distance from the guards Tarzan paused and faced his visitor. "What is it?" he asked. "You have brought me bad news?"

"Very bad," replied Phobeg. "Gemnon, Thudos, and many of their friends have been arrested and are now in the palace dungeons. Doria has been taken and is imprisoned in the temple. I did not expect to find you at liberty, but took the chance that Nemone's interest in you might have saved you temporarily. If you can escape from Cathne, do so at once; her mood may change at any moment; she is as mad as a monkey."

"Thank you, Phobeg," said the ape-man. "Now get back to your quarters before you become embroiled in this affair."

"And you will escape?" asked the warrior.

"I owe something to Gemnon," replied Tarzan, "for his kindness and his friendship; so I shall not go until I have done what I can to help him."

"No one can help him," stated Phobeg emphatically. "All that you will do is get yourself in trouble."

"I shall have to chance it, and now goodbye, my friend; but before you go tell me where Doria is imprisoned."

"On the third floor of the temple at the rear of the building just above the doorway where I awaited you this evening."

Tarzan accompanied Phobeg to the gate and out into the avenue. "Where are you going?" demanded the latter.

"To the palace."

"You, too, are mad," protested Phobeg, but already the ape-man had left him and was walking rapidly along the avenue in the direction of the palace.

It was late; but Tarzan was now a familiar figure to the palace guards; and when he told them that Nemone had summoned him they let him enter, nor was he stopped until he had reached the anteroom outside the Queen's apartments. Here a noble on guard protested that the hour was late and that the Queen had retired, but Tarzan insisted upon seeing her.

"Tell her it is Tarzan," he said.

"I do not dare disturb her," explained the noble nervously, fearful of Nemone's wrath should she be disturbed and almost equally fearful of it should he refuse to announce this new favorite who had replaced Erot.

"I dare," said Tarzan and stepped to the door leading to the ivory room where Nemone had been accustomed to receive him. The noble sought to interfere but the ape-man pushed him aside and attempted to open the door only to find it securely bolted upon the opposite side; then with his clenched fist he pounded loudly upon its carved surface.

Instantly from beyond it came the savage growls of Belthar and a moment later the frightened voice of a woman. "Who is there?" she demanded. "The Queen sleeps. Who dares disturb her?"

"Go and awaken her," shouted Tarzan through the door. "Tell her that Tarzan is here and wishes to see her at once."

"I am afraid," replied the girl. "The Queen will be angry. Go away, and come in the morning."

Then Tarzan heard another voice beyond the door demanding, "Who is it comes pounding on Nemone's door at such an hour?" and recognized it as the Queen's.

"It is the noble Tarzan," replied the slave girl.

"Draw the bolts and admit him," commanded Nemone, and as the door swung open Tarzan stepped into the ivory room, now so familiar to him.

The Queen stood halfway across the apartment, facing him. Her hair was dishevelled, her face slightly flushed. She had evidently arisen from her bed in an adjoining room and thrown a light scarf about her before stepping into the ivory room. She was very beautiful. There was an eager, questioning light in her eyes. She directed the slave to rebolt the door and leave the apartment; then she turned and, walking to the couch, motioned Tarzan to approach. As she sank among the soft cushions she motioned Tarzan to her side.

"I am glad you came," she said. "I could not sleep. I have been thinking of you. But tell me! why did you come? Had you been thinking of me?"

"I have been thinking of you, Nemone," replied the ape-man; "I have been thinking that perhaps you will help me; that you can help me, I know."

"You have only to ask," replied the Queen softly. "There is

no favor that you may not have from Nemone for the asking."

A single cresset shed a soft, flickering light that scarcely dispelled the darkness of the room, at the far end of which the yellow-green eyes of Belthar blazed like twin lamps of Hell. Mingling with the acrid scent of the carnivore and the languorous fumes of incense was the seductive aura of the scented body of the woman. Her warm breath was on Tarzan's cheek as she drew him down beside her.

"At last you have come to me of your own volition," she whispered. "Ah, Thoos! how I have hungered for this moment!"

Her soft, bare arms slipped quickly about his neck and drew him close. "Tarzan! My Tarzan!" she almost sobbed, and then that same fatal door at the far end of the apartment opened and the tapping of a metal-shod staff upon the stone floor brought them both erect to gaze into the snarling face of M'duze.

"You fool!" cried the old hag in a shrill falsetto. "Send the man away! unless you would see him killed here before your eyes. Send him away at once!"

Nemone sprang to her feet and faced the old woman who was now trembling with rage. "You have gone too far, M'duze," she said in a cold and level voice. "Go to your room, and remember that I am Queen."

"Queen! Queen!" cackled the hideous creature with a sharp, sarcastic laugh. "Send your lover away, or I'll tell him who and what you are."

Nemone glided quickly toward her, and as she passed a low stand she stooped and seized something that lay there. Suddenly the slave woman shrieked and shrank away, but before she could turn and flee Nemone was upon her and had seized her by the hair. M'duze raised her staff and struck at the Queen, but the blow only aroused the frenzied woman to still greater fury.

"Always you have ruined my life," cried Nemone, "you and your foul paramour, Tomos. You have robbed me of happiness, and for that, *this!*" and she drove the gleaming blade of a knife into the withered breast of the screaming woman, "and this, and this, and this!" and each time the blade sank deep to emphasize the venom in the words and the heart of Nemone, the queen.

Presently M'duze ceased shrieking and sank to the floor. Someone was pounding upon the door to the anteroom, and the terrified voices of nobles and guardsmen could be heard demanding entrance. In his corner Belthar tugged at his chains and roared. Nemone stood looking down upon the death struggles of M'duze with blazing eyes and snarling lip. "Curses upon your black soul!" she cried, and then she turned slowly toward the door upon which the pounding of her retainers' fists resounded. "Have done!" she called imperiously. "I, Nemone, the Queen, am safe. The screams that you heard were those of an impudent slave whom Nemone was correcting."

The voices beyond the door died away as the guardsmen returned to their posts; then Nemone faced Tarzan. She looked suddenly worn and very tired. "That favor," she said, "ask it another time; Nemone is unstrung."

"I must ask it now," replied Tarzan; "tomorrow may be too late."

"Very well," she said; "I am listening. What is it?"

"There is a noble in your court who has been very kind to me since I have been in Cathne," commenced Tarzan. "Now he is in trouble, and I have come to ask you to save him."

Nemone's brow clouded. "Who is he?" she demanded.

"Gemnon," replied the ape-man. "He has been arrested with Thudos and the daughter of Thudos and several of their friends. It is only a plot to destroy me."

"You dare come to me to intercede for traitors!" cried the Queen, blazing with sudden fury. "But I know the reason; you love Doria!"

"I do not love her; I have seen her but once. Gemnon loves her. Let them be happy, Nemone."

"I am not happy," she replied; "why should they be happy? Tell me that you love me, Tarzan, and I shall be happy!" Her voice was vibrant with appeal. For a moment she forgot that she was queen.

"A flower does not bloom in the seed," he replied; "it grows gradually, and thus love grows. The other, that bursts forth spontaneously from its own heat, is not love; it is passion. I have not known you either long or well, Nemone; that is my answer."

She turned away and buried her face in her arms as she

sank to the couch; he saw her shoulders shaken by sobs, and pity filled his heart. He drew nearer to console her, but he had no chance to speak before she wheeled upon him, her eyes flashing through tears. "The girl, Doria, dies!" she cried. "Xarator shall have her tomorrow!"

Tarzan shook his head sadly. "You have asked me to love you," he said. "Do you expect me to love one who ruthlessly destroys my friends?"

"If I save them will you love me?" demanded Nemone.

"That is a question that I cannot answer. The best that I may say is that I may then respect and admire you; whereas, if you kill them without reason there can be no chance that I shall ever love you."

She looked at him now out of dull, lowering eyes. "What difference does it make?" she almost growled. "No one loves me. Tomos wanted to be king, Erot wished riches and power, M'duze wished to exercise the majesty that she could never possess; if one of them felt any affection for me it was M'duze, and I have killed her." She paused, a wild light flamed in her eyes. "I hate them!" she screamed. "I hate them all! I shall kill them! I shall kill every one! I shall kill you!" Then, as swiftly, her mood changed. "Oh, what am I saying?" she cried. She put her palms to her temples. "My head! it hurts."

"And my friends!" asked Tarzan; "you will not harm them?"

"Perhaps not," she replied indifferently, and then, as quickly changing again, "The girl dies! If you intercede for her again her sufferings shall be greater; Xarator is merciful —more merciful than Nemone."

"When will she die?" asked Tarzan.

"She will be sewn into hides tonight and carried to Xarator tomorrow. You shall accompany us; do you understand?"

The ape-man nodded. "And my other friends?" he asked, "they will be saved?"

"You shall come to me tomorrow night," replied Nemone. "We shall see then how you have decided to treat Nemone; then she will know how to treat your friends."

18

Flaming Xarator

H ER wrists and ankles bound, Doria, the daughter of Thudos, lay on a pile of skins in a room upon the third floor of the Temple of Thoos. Diffused moonlight entered the single window, relieving the darkness of the interior of her prison. She had seen her father seized and dragged away; she was in the power of one so ruthless that she knew she could expect no mercy and that either death or cruel disfigurement awaited her, yet she did not weep. Above her grief rose the pride of the noble blood of the house of Thudos, the courage of a line of warriors that stretched back into the forgotten ages; and she was brave.

She thought of Gemnon; and then the tears almost came, not for herself but for him because of the grief that would be his when he learned of her fate. She did not know that he too had fallen into the clutches of the enemies of her father.

Presently she heard the sound of footsteps approaching along the corridor, heard them stop before the door behind which she was locked. The door swung open and the room was illuminated by the light of a torch held in the hand of a man who entered and closed the door behind him.

The girl lying upon the pile of skins recognized Erot. She saw him place the blazing torch in a wall socket designed for the purpose and turn toward her.

"Ah, the lovely Doria!" he exclaimed. "What ill fate has brought you here?"

"Doubtless the noble Erot could answer that question better than I," she replied.

"Yes, I believe that he could; in fact I know it. It was I who caused you to be brought here; it was I who caused your father to be imprisoned; it was I who sent Gemnon to the same cell with the noble Thudos."

"Gemnon imprisoned!" cried the girl.

"Yes, with many other conspirators against the throne. Behind his back they used to sneer at Erot because he was not a lion man; they will not sneer for long. Erot has answered them; now they know that Erot is more powerful than they."

"And what is to be done with me?" asked the girl.

"Nemone has decreed Xarator for you," replied Erot. "You are even now lying upon the skins in which you are to be sewn. It is for that purpose that I am here. My good friend Tomos, the councillor, sent me to sew you into the bag; but first let us enjoy together your last night on earth. Be generous, and perhaps I can avert the doom that Nemone will doubtless decree for your father and your lover. She is permitting them to live through tomorrow at least, that they may witness your destruction, for thus runs the kindly mind of sweet Nemone." He laughed harshly. "The hell-cat! May the devil get her in the end!"

"You have not even the decency of gratitude," said Doria contemptuously. "The Queen has lavished favors upon you, given you power and riches; it is inconceivable that one can be so vile an ingrate as you."

Erot laughed. "Tomorrow you will be dead," he said; "so what difference does it make what you think of me? Tonight you shall give me love, though your heart be filled with hate. There is nothing in the world but love and hate, the two most pleasurable emotions that great Thoos has given us; let us enjoy them to the full!" He came and kneeled at her side and took her in his arms, covering her face and lips with kisses. She struggled to repulse him, but in her bonds she was helpless to protect herself.

He was panting with passion as he untied the thongs that secured her ankles. "You are more beautiful than Nemone," he cried huskily as he strained her to him.

A low growl sounded from the direction of the window. Erot raised his face from the soft neck of Doria and looked.

He went ashy white as he leaped to his feet and fled toward the door upon the opposite side of the room, his craven heart pounding in terror.

*   *   *

It was early in the morning as the *cortège* formed that was to accompany the doomed Doria to Xarator, for Xarator lies sixteen miles from the city of Cathne in the mountains at the far end of the valley of Onthar; and the procession could move no faster than the lions drawing the chariot of the Queen would walk, which was not fast. Bred for generations for this purpose, the lions of Cathne had far greater endurance than forest-bred lions, yet it would be well into the night before it could be hoped to make the long journey to Xarator and return; therefore hundreds of slaves bore torches with which to light the homeward journey after night had fallen.

Nemone entered her chariot. She was wrapped in woolen robes and the skins of animals, for the morning air was still chill. At her side walked Tomos, nervous and ill at ease. He knew that M'duze was dead and wondered if he would be next. The Queen's manner was curt and abrupt, filling him with dread, for now there was no M'duze to protect him from the easily aroused wrath of Nemone.

"Where is Tarzan?" she demanded.

"I do not know, majesty," replied Tomos. "I have not seen him."

She looked at him sharply. "Don't lie to me!" she snapped. "You do know where he is; and if any harm has befallen him, you go to the lion pit."

"But, majesty," cried Tomos, "I know nothing about him. I have not seen him since we left the temple yesterday."

"Produce him," commanded Nemone sullenly. "It grows late, and Nemone is not accustomed to wait upon any."

"But, majesty—" began Tomos again.

"Produce him!" interrupted Nemone.

"But——"

"Here he comes now!" exclaimed Nemone as Tarzan strode up the avenue toward her.

Tomos breathed a sigh of relief and wiped the perspiration from his forehead. He did not like Tarzan, but in all his life he had never before been so glad to see anyone alive and well.

"You are late," said Nemone as Tarzan stopped beside her chariot.

The lord of the jungle made no reply.

"We are not accustomed to being delayed," she continued a little sharply.

"Perhaps if you placed me in the custody of Erot, as I suggested, he would deliver me on time in future."

Nemone ignored this and turned to Tomos. "We are ready," she said.

At a word from the councillor a trumpeter at his side raised his instrument to his lips and sounded a call. Slowly the long procession began to move, and like a huge serpent crawled toward the Bridge of Gold. The citizens lining the avenue moved with it, men, women, and children. The women and children carried packages in which food was wrapped, the men bore arms. A journey to Xarator was an event; it took them the length of Onthar where wild lions roamed and where Athnean raiders might set upon them at any moment of the day or night, especially of the night; so the march took on something of the aspects of both a pageant and a military excursion.

Behind the golden chariot of the Queen rolled a second chariot on the floor of which lay a bundle sewn in the skins of lions. Chained to this chariot were Thudos and Gemnon. Following were a hundred chariots driven by nobles in gold and ivory, while other nobles on foot entirely surrounded the chariot of the Queen.

There were columns of marching warriors in the lead; and in the rear were the war lions of Cathne, the royal fighting lions of the Queen. Keepers held them on leashes of gold, and proud nobles of ancient families marched beside them—the lion men of Cathne.

The barbaric splendor of the scene impressed even the ape-man who cared little for display, though he gave no outward sign of interest as he strode at the wheel of Nemone's chariot drawn by its eight great lions held in leash by twenty-four powerful blacks in tunics of red and gold.

The comments of the crowd came to the ears of Tarzan as they marched through the city and out across the Bridge of Gold onto the road that runs north through the Field of

the Lions. "There is the stranger who defeated Phobeg."
"Yes, he has taken Erot's place in the council." "He is the
Queen's favorite now." "Where is Erot?" "I hope he is dead;
this other is better." "He will soon be as bad; they all get
alike when they get rich and powerful." "Had you heard the
rumor that M'duze is dead?" "She *is* dead; my cousin's husband is a palace guard. He told my cousin." "What is
that?" "M'duze is dead!" "May Thoos be praised!" "Have
you heard? M'duze is dead!" and so it ran through the two
streams of citizens that hemmed the royal pageant on either
side, and always above the other comment rose the half
exultant cry, "M'duze is dead!"

Nemone appeared preoccupied; she sat staring straight
ahead; if she heard the comments of her people she gave no
sign. What was passing behind that beautiful mask that
was her face? Chained to the chariot behind her were two
enemies; others were in her prisons. A girl who dared vie
with her in beauty lay insensible in a sack of skins jolting
over the rough road in the dust of the Queen's chariot. Her
Nemesis was dead. The man she loved walked at her side.
Nemone should have been happy; but she was not.

The sun, climbing into the heavens, was bringing heat.
Slaves carrying an umbrella over the Queen adjusted it to
fend the hot rays from her; others waved lions' tails attached to the ends of long poles to and fro about her to
drive the insects away; a gentle breeze carried the dust of
the long column lazily toward the west.

Nemone sighed and turned to Tarzan. "Why were you late?"
she asked.

"Would it be strange that I overslept?" he asked. "It was
late when I left the palace, and there was no keeper to
awaken me since you took Gemnon away."

"Had you wished to see me again as badly as I wished
to see you, you would not have been late."

"I was as anxious to be here as you," he replied.

"You have never seen Xarator?" she asked.

"No."

"It is a holy mountain, created by Thoos for the enemies of
the kings and queens of Cathne; in all the world there is
nothing like it."

"I am going to enjoy seeing it," replied the ape-man
grimly.

They were approaching a fork in the road. "That road leading to the right runs through the Pass of the Warriors into the valley of Thenar," she explained. "Some day I shall send you on a raid to Thenar, and you shall bring me back the head of one of Athne's greatest warriors."

Tarzan thought of Valthor and wondered if he had reached Athne in safety. He glanced back at Thudos and Gemnon. He had not spoken to them, but it was because of them that he was here. He might easily have escaped had he not determined to remain until he was certain that he could not aid these friends. Their case appeared hopeless, yet the ape-man had not given up hope.

At noon the procession stopped for lunch. The populace scattered about seeking the shade of the trees that dotted the plain and that had not already been selected by the Queen and the nobles. The lions were led into shade, where they lay down to rest. Warriors, always on the lookout for danger, stood guard about the temporary encampment. There was always danger on the Field of the Lions.

The halt was brief; in half an hour the cavalcade was on the march again. There was less talking now; silence and the great heat hung over the dusty column. The hills that bounded the valley upon the north were close, and soon they entered them, following a canyon upward to a winding mountain road that led into the hills above.

Presently the smell of sulphur fumes came plainly to the nostrils of the ape-man, and a little later the column turned the shoulder of a great mass of volcanic rock and came upon the edge of a huge crater. Far below, molten rock bubbled, sending up spurts of flame, geysers of steam, and columns of yellow smoke. The scene was impressive and awe-inspiring. Before Cathne, before Rome, before Athens, before Babylon, before Egypt Xarator had towered in lonely majesty above the lesser peaks. Beside that mighty cauldron queen and noble shrank to pitiful insignificance though perhaps there was but one in that great throng that realized this. Tarzan stood with folded arms and bent head gazing down into the seething inferno until the Queen touched him on the shoulder. "What do you think of Xarator?" she asked.

He shook his head. "There are some emotions," he answered slowly, "for which no words have yet been coined."

"It was created by Thoos for the kings of Cathne," she explained proudly.

Tarzan made no reply; perhaps he was thinking that here again the lexicographers had failed to furnish words adequate to the occasion.

On either side of the royal party the people crowded close to the edge of the crater that they might miss nothing of what was about to transpire. The children laughed and played, or teased their mothers for the food that was being saved for the evening meal upon the return journey to Cathne.

Tarzan saw Thudos and Gemnon standing beside the chariot in which lay the still form of the victim. Of what emotions were passing within their minds none appeared through the masks of stern pride that sat upon their countenances, yet Tarzan well knew the suffering of their torn and bleeding hearts. He had not spoken to them once this day, for he had not had an opportunity to speak to them except in the presence of others; and whatever he might have to say to them must be for their ears only. He had not given up the hope of helping them, but he could not conceive that open and unnecessary familiarity with them at this time might accomplish anything more than to still further arouse the suspicions of Nemone and increase the watchfulness of all their enemies.

If Gemnon or Thudos noticed the neglect of their former friend and guest they gave no sign, for neither gave him any greater attention as he walked beside the chariot of the Queen a few paces in advance of them than they gave to the lions drawing the car to which they were secured. Their thoughts were upon the poor, dumb thing jolting upon the hard planks that formed the floor of the springless chariot bearing it to its doom. Not once had they seen the girl move, not once had she uttered a sound; and they hoped that she was either insensible or dead, for thus would she be saved the anguish of these last moments and Nemone be robbed of the essence of her triumph.

The ceremony at Xarator, though it bore the authority of so-called justice, was of a semi-religious nature that required the presence and active participation of priests, two of whom lifted the sack containing the victim from the chariot and placed it at the edge of the crater at the feet of the Queen.

About it, then, gathered a dozen priests, some of whom carried musical instruments; and as they chanted in unison, the beating of their drums rose and fell while the wailing notes of their wind instruments floated out across the inferno of the seething pit like the plaint of a lost soul.

Thudos and Gemnon had been brought nearer the spot that Nemone might enjoy their agony to the full, for this was not only a part of their punishment but a considerable portion of the pleasure of the Queen.

She saw that they were giving no evidences of grief, thus robbing her of much of the satisfaction she had hoped to derive from the destruction of the daughter of one, the sweetheart of the other; and she was vexed. But she was not entirely discouraged; a new plan to further try their fortitude had occurred to her.

As two of the priests lifted the body from the ground and were about to hurl it into the crater, she stopped them with a curt command. "Wait!" she cried. "We would look upon the too great beauty of Doria, the daughter of Thudos, the traitor; we would permit her father and her lover to see her once again that they may better visualize her anguish and appreciate their own; that all may long remember that it is not well to conspire against Nemone. Cut the bag, and expose the body of the sacrifice!"

All eyes were upon the priest who drew his dagger and ripped open the bag along one loosely sewn seam. The eyes of Thudos and Gemnon were fixed upon the still figure outlined beneath the tawny skins of lions; beads of perspiration stood upon their foreheads; their jaws and their fists were clenched. The eyes of Tarzan turned from the activities of the priest to the face of the Queen; between narrowed lids, from beneath stern brows they watched her.

The priests, gathering the bag by one side, raised it and let the body roll out upon the ground where all could see it. There was a gasp of astonishment. Nemone cried out in a sudden fit of rage. The body was that of Erot, and he was dead!

19

The Queen's Quarry

A FTER the first involuntary cries of surprise and rage an ominous silence fell upon the barbaric scene. Now all eyes were centered upon the Queen, whose ordinarily beautiful countenance was almost hideous from rage, a rage which, after her single angry cry, choked further utterance for the moment. But at length she found her voice and turned furiously upon Tomos.

"What means this?" she demanded, her voice now controlled and as cold as the steel in the sheath at her side.

Tomos, who was as much astounded as she, stammered as he trembled in his sandals of elephant hide. "There are traitors even in the temple of Thoos!" he cried. "I chose Erot to prepare the girl for the embraces of Xarator because I knew that his loyalty to his Queen would insure the work being well done. I did not know, O gracious Nemone, that this vile crime had been committed or that the body of Erot had been substituted for that of the daughter of Thudos until this very instant."

With an expression of disgust the Queen commanded the priests to hurl the body of Erot into the crater, and as it was swallowed by the fiery pit she ordered an immediate return to Cathne.

In morose and gloomy silence she rode down the winding mountain trail and out onto the Field of the Lions, and often her eyes were upon the bronzed giant striding beside her chariot.

At last she broke her silence. "Two of your enemies are

gone now," she said. "I destroyed one; whom do you think destroyed the other?"

"Perhaps I did," suggested Tarzan with a smile.

"I had been thinking of that possibility," replied Nemone, but she did not smile.

"Whoever did it performed a service for Cathne."

"Perhaps," she half agreed, "but it is not the killing of Erot that annoys me; it is the effrontery that dared interfere with the plans of Nemone. Whoever did it has spoiled for me what would otherwise have been a happy day; nor have they accomplished anything in the interest of Thudos or his daughter or Gemnon. I shall find the girl, and her passing will be far more bitter than that from which she was saved today; she cannot escape me. Thudos and Gemnon will also pay more heavily because some one dared flout the Queen."

Tarzan shrugged his broad shoulders, but remained silent.

"Why do you not speak?" demanded the Queen.

"There is nothing to say," he replied; "I can only disagree with you without convincing you; I should only make you more angry than you are. I find no pleasure in making people angry or unhappy unless it is for some good purpose."

"You mean that I do?" she demanded.

"Obviously."

She shook her head angrily. "Why do I abide you!" she exclaimed.

"Possibly as a counterirritant to relieve other irritations," he suggested.

"Some day I shall lose my patience and have you thrown to the lions," she ejaculated sharply. "What will you do then?"

"Kill the lion," replied the ape-man.

"Not the lion that I shall throw you to," Nemone assured him.

The tedious journey back to Cathne ended at last, and with flaring torches lighting the way the Queen's *cortège* crossed the Bridge of Gold and entered the city. Here she immediately ordered a thorough search to be made for Doria.

Thudos and Gemnon, happy but mystified, were returned to their cell to await the new doom that Nemone would fix for them when the mood again seized her to be entertained. Tarzan was commanded to accompany Nemone into the palace and dine with her. Tomos had been dismissed with a curt injunction to find Doria or prepare for the worst!

Tarzan and the Queen ate alone in a small dining room attended only by slaves, and when the meal was over Nemone conducted him to the now all too familiar ivory room, where he was greeted by the angry growls of Belthar.

"Erot and M'duze are dead," said the Queen, "and I have sent Tomos away; there will be none to disturb us tonight." Again her voice was soft, her manner gentle.

The ape-man sat with his eyes fixed upon her, studying her. It seemed incredible that this sweet and lovely woman could be the cruel tyrant that was Nemone, the Queen. Every soft line and curving contour spoke of femininity and gentleness and love; and in those glorious eyes smoldered a dreamy light that exercised a strange hypnotic influence upon him, gently pushing the memories of her ruthlessness into the oblivion of forgetfulness.

She leaned closer to him. "Touch me, Tarzan," she whispered softly.

Drawn by a power that is greater than the will of man he placed a hand upon hers. She breathed a deep sigh of contentment and leaned her cheek against his breast; her warm breath caressed his naked skin; the perfume of her hair was in his nostrils. She spoke, but so low that he could not catch her words.

"What did you say?" he asked.

"Take me in your arms," she breathed faintly.

He passed a palm across his eyes as though to wipe away a mist, and in the moment of his hesitation she threw her arms about his neck and covered his face and lips with hot kisses.

"Love me, Tarzan!" she cried passionately. "Love me! Love me! Love me!"

She slipped to the floor until she knelt at his feet. "Oh, Thoos, god of gods!" she murmured, "how I love you!"

The lord of the jungle looked down at her, at a queen grovelling at his feet, and the spell that had held him vanished; beneath the beautiful exterior he saw the crazed mind of a mad woman; he saw the creature that cast defenseless men to wild beasts, that disfigured or destroyed women who might be more beautiful than she; and all that was fine in him revolted.

With a half growl he arose to his feet, and as he did so Nemone slipped to the floor and lay there silent and rigid. He started toward the door, and then turned and coming back lifted her to the couch. As he did so, Belthar strained at his chains and the chamber shook to his roars.

Nemone opened her eyes and for a moment gazed questioningly at the man above her; then she seemed to realize what had happened, and the mad, cruel light of rage blazed in her eyes. Leaping to her feet she stood trembling before him.

"You refuse my love!" she screamed. "You spurn me? You dare spurn the love of a Queen! Thoos! and I knelt at your feet!" She sprang to one side of the room where a metal gong depended from the ceiling and seizing the striker smote it three times. The brazen notes rang through the chamber mingling with the roars of the infuriated lion.

Tarzan stood watching her; she seemed wholly irresponsible, quite mad. It would be useless to attempt to reason with her. He moved slowly toward the door; but before he reached it it swung open, and a score of warriors accompanied by two nobles rushed in.

"Take this man!" ordered Nemone. "Throw him into the cell with the other enemies of the Queen!"

Tarzan was unarmed. He had worn only a sword when he entered the ivory room and that he had unbuckled and laid upon a stand near the doorway. There were twenty spears levelled at him, twenty spears that entirely encircled him. With a shrug he surrendered. It was that or death. In prison he might find the means to escape; at least he would see Gemnon again, and there was something that he very much wished to tell Gemnon and Thudos.

As the soldiers conducted him from the room and the door closed behind them, Nemone threw herself among the cushions of her couch, her body wracked by choking sobs. The great lion grumbled in the dusky corner of the room. Suddenly Nemone sat erect and her eyes blazed into the blazing eyes of the lion. For a moment she sat there thus, and then she arose and a peal of maniacal laughter broke from her lips. Still laughing, she crossed the room and passed through the doorway that led to her bedchamber.

Thudos and Gemnon sitting in their cell heard the tramp of marching men approaching the prison in which they were confined. "Evidently Nemone cannot wait until tomorrow," said Thudos.

"You think she is sending for us now?" asked Gemnon.

"What else?" demanded the older man. "The lion pit can be illuminated."

As they waited and listened the steps stopped outside their cell, the door was pushed open, and a man entered. The warriors had carried no torches and neither Thudos nor Gemnon could discern the features of the newcomer, though in the diffused light that filtered in through the small window and the aperture in the door they noted that he was a large man.

None of them spoke until the guard had departed out of earshot. "Greetings, Thudos and Gemnon!" exclaimed the new prisoner cheerily.

"Tarzan!" exclaimed Gemnon.

"None other," admitted the ape-man.

"What brings you here?" demanded Thudos.

"Twenty warriors and the whim of a woman, an insane woman," replied Tarzan.

"So you have fallen from favor!" exclaimed Gemnon. "I am sorry."

"It was inevitable," said Tarzan.

"And what will your punishment be?"

"I do not know, but I suspect that it will be quite sufficient. However, that is something that need not concern any of us until it happens; maybe it won't happen."

"There is no room in the dungeon of Nemone for optimism," remarked Thudos with a grim laugh.

"Perhaps not," agreed the ape-man, "but I shall continue to indulge myself. Doubtless Doria felt hopeless in her prison in the temple last night, yet she escaped Xarator."

"That is a miracle that I cannot fathom," said Gemnon.

"It was quite simple," Tarzan assured him. "A loyal friend, whose identity you may guess, came and told me that she was a prisoner in the temple. I went at once to find her. Fortunately the trees of Cathne are old and large and numerous; one of them grows close to the rear of the temple, its branches almost brushing the window of the room in which Doria was confined. When I arrived there, I found Erot annoying Doria; I also found the sack in which he had purposed tying her for the journey to Xarator. What was sim-

pler? I let Erot take the ride that had been planned for'
Doria."

"You saved her! Where is she?" cried Thudos, his voice
breaking in the first emotion he had displayed since he had
learned of his daughter's plight.

"Come close," cautioned Tarzan, "lest the walls themselves
be enemies." The two men pressed close to the speaker who
continued in a low whisper, "Do you recall, Gemnon, that
when we were at the gold mine I spoke aside to one of the
slaves there?"

"I believe that I did notice it," replied Gemnon; "I thought
you were asking questions about the operation of the mine."

"No; I was delivering a message from his brother, and
so grateful was he that he begged that he be permitted to
serve me if the opportunity arose. It was to arise much sooner
than either of us could have expected; and so, when it was
necessary to find a hiding place for Doria, I thought immediately of the isolated hut of Niaka, the headman of the black
slaves at the gold mine.

"She is there now, and the man will protect her as long
as is necessary. He has promised me that if he hears nothing
from me for half a moon he is to understand that none of
us three can come to her aid, and that then he will get word
to the faithful slaves of the house of Thudos. He says that
that will be difficult but not impossible."

"Doria safe!" whispered Gemnon. "Thudos and I may
now die happy."

Thudos extended his hand through the darkness and laid
it on the ape-man's shoulder. "There is no way in which I
can express my gratitude," he said, "for there are no words
in which to couch it."

For some time the three men sat in silence that was
broken at last by Gemnon. "How did it happen that you
knew the brother of a slave well enough to carry a message
from one to the other?" he asked, a note of puzzlement in
his voice.

"Do you recall Xerstle's grand hunt?" asked Tarzan with
a laugh.

"Of course, but what has that to do with it?" demanded
Gemnon.

"Do you remember the quarry, the man we saw on the
slave block in the market place?"

"Yes."

"He is the brother of Niaka," explained Tarzan.

"But you never had an opportunity to speak to him," objected the young noble.

"Oh, but I did. It was I who helped him escape. That was why his brother was so grateful to me."

"I still do not understand," said Gemnon.

"There is probably much connected with Xerstle's grand hunt that you do not understand," suggested Tarzan. "In the first place, the purpose of the hunt was, primarily, to destroy me rather than the nominal quarry; the scheme was probably hatched between Xerstle and Erot. In the second place, I didn't approve of the ethics of the hunters; the poor devil they were chasing had no chance. I went ahead, therefore, through the trees until I overtook the black; then I carried him for a mile to throw the lions off the scent. You know how well the plan succeeded.

"When I came back and we laid the wager, that gave Xerstle and Pindes the opening they wished but which they would have found by some other means before the day was over; so Pindes took me with him; and after we were far enough away from you he suggested that we separate, whereupon he loosed his lion upon me."

"And it was you who killed the lion?"

"I should have much preferred to have killed Pindes and Xerstle, but I felt that the time was not yet ripe. Now, perhaps, I shall never have the opportunity to kill them," he added regretfully.

"Now I am doubly sorry that I must die," said Gemnon.

"Why more so than before?" asked Thudos.

"I shall never have the opportunity to tell the story of Xerstle's grand hunt," he explained. "What a story *that* would make!"

The morning dawned bright and beautiful, just as though there was no misery or sorrow or cruelty in the world; but it did not change matters at all, other than to make the cell in which the three men were confined uncomfortably warm as the day progressed.

Shortly after noon a guard came and took Tarzan away. All three of the prisoners were acquainted with the officer who commanded it, a decent fellow who spoke sympathetically to them.

"Is he coming back?" asked Thudos, nodding toward Tarzan.

The officer shook his head. "No; the Queen hunts today."

Thudos and Gemnon pressed the ape-man's shoulder. No word was spoken, but that wordless farewell was more eloquent than words. They saw him go out, saw the door close behind him; but neither spoke, and so they sat for a long hour in silence.

In the guardroom, to which he had been conducted from his cell, Tarzan was heavily chained; a golden collar was placed about his neck, and a chain reaching from each side of it was held in the hands of a warrior.

"Why all the precautions?" demanded the ape-man.

"It is merely a custom," explained the officer; "it is always thus that the Queen's quarry is led to the Field of the Lions."

Once again Tarzan of the Apes walked near the chariot of the Queen of Cathne; but this time he walked behind it, a chained prisoner between two stalwart warriors and surrounded by a score of others. Once again he crossed the Bridge of Gold out onto the Field of the Lions in the valley of Onthar.

The procession did not go far, scarcely more than a mile from the city. A great concourse of people accompanied it, for Nemone had invited the entire city to witness the degradation and death of the man who had spurned her love. She was about to be avenged, but she was not happy. With scowling brows she sat brooding in her chariot as it stopped at last at the point she had selected for the start of the hunt. Not once had she turned to look at the chained man behind her. Perhaps she had been certain that she would have been rewarded by no indication of terror in his mien, or perhaps she did not dare to look at the man she had loved for fear that her determination might weaken.

But now that the time had come she cast her indecision aside, if any had been annoying her, and ordered the guard to fetch the prisoner to her. She was looking straight ahead as the ape-man halted by the wheel of her chariot.

"Send all away except the two warriors who hold him," commanded Nemone.

"You may send them, too, if you wish," said Tarzan; "I

give you my word not to harm you or try to escape while they are away."

Nemone, still looking straight ahead, was silent for a moment; then, "You may all go; I would speak with the prisoner alone."

When the guard had departed a number of paces, the Queen turned her eyes toward Tarzan and found his smiling into her own. "You are going to be very happy, Nemone," he said in an easy, friendly voice.

"What do you mean?" she asked. "How am I going to be happy?"

"You are going to see me die; that is if the lion catches me," he laughed, "and you like to see people die."

"You think that will give me pleasure? Well, I thought so myself; but now I am wondering if it will. I never get quite the pleasure from death that I anticipate I shall; nothing in life is ever what I hope for."

"Possibly you don't hope for the right things," he suggested. "Did you ever try hoping for something that would bring pleasure and happiness to someone beside yourself?"

"Why should I?" she asked. "I hope for my own happiness; let others do the same. I strive for my own happiness——"

"And never have any," interrupted the ape-man good-naturedly.

"Probably I should have less if I strove only for the happiness of others," she insisted.

"There are people like that," he assented; "perhaps you are one of them; so you might as well go on striving for happiness in your own way. Of course you won't get it, but you will at least have the pleasures of anticipation, and that is something."

"I think I know myself and my own affairs well enough to determine for myself how to conduct my life," she said with a note of asperity in her voice.

Tarzan shrugged. "It was not in my thoughts to interfere," he said. "If you are determined to kill me and are quite sure that you will derive pleasure from it, why, I should be the last in the world to suggest that you abandon the idea."

"You do not amuse me," said Nemone haughtily; "I do not care for irony that is aimed at myself." She turned fiercely on him. "Men have died for less!" she cried, and the lord of the jungle laughed in her face.

"How many times?" he asked.

"A moment ago," said Nemone, "I was beginning to regret the thing that is about to happen. Had you been different, had you sought to conciliate me, I might have relented and returned you to favor; but you do everything to antagonize me. You affront me, you insult me, you laugh at me." Her voice was rising, a barometric indication, Tarzan had learned, of her mental state.

"And yet, Nemone, I am drawn to you," admitted the apeman. "I cannot understand it. You are attracted to me in spite of wounded pride and lacerated dignity; and I to you though I hold in contempt your principles, your ideals, and your methods. It is strange, isn't it?"

The woman nodded. "It is strange," she mused. "I never loved one as I loved you, and yet I am going to kill you notwithstanding the fact that I still love you."

"And you will go on killing people and being unhappy until it is your turn to be killed," he said sadly.

She shuddered. "Killed!" she repeated. "Yes, they are all killed, the kings and queens of Cathne; but it is not my turn yet. While Belthar lives Nemone lives." She was silent for a moment. "You may live too, Tarzan; there is something that I would rather see you do than see you die." She paused as though expecting him to ask her what it was, but he manifested no interest, and she continued, "Last night I knelt at your feet and begged for your love. Kneel here, before my people, kneel at my feet and beg for mercy, and you may live."

"Bring on your lion," said Tarzan; "his mercy might be kinder than Nemone's."

"You refuse?" she demanded angrily.

"You would kill me eventually," he replied; "there is a chance that the lion may not be able to."

"Not a chance!" she said. "Have you seen the lion?"

"No."

She turned and called a noble, "Have the hunting lion brought to scent the quarry!"

Behind them there was a scattering of troops and nobles as they made an avenue for the hunting lion and his keepers, and along the avenue Tarzan saw a great lion straining at the golden leashes to which eight men clung. Growling and roaring, the beast sprang from side to side in an effort to seize a keeper or lay hold upon one of the warriors or nobles that lined the way; so that it was all that four stalwart men on either side of him could do to prevent his accomplishing his design.

A flaming-eyed devil, he came toward the chariot of Nemone, but he was still afar when Tarzan saw the tuft of white hair in the center of his mane between his ears. It was Belthar!

Nemone was eyeing the man at her side as a cat might eye a mouse, but though the lion was close now she saw no change in the expression on Tarzan's face. "Do you not recognize him?" she demanded.

"Of course I do," he replied.

"And you are not afraid?"

"Of what?" he asked, looking at her wonderingly.

She stamped her foot in anger, thinking that he was trying to rob her of the satisfaction of witnessing his terror; for how could she know that Tarzan of the Apes could not understand the meaning of *fear?* "Prepare for the grand hunt!" she commanded, turning to a noble standing with the guard that had waited just out of earshot of her conversation with the quarry.

The warriors who had held Tarzan in leash ran forward and picked up the golden chains that were attached to the golden collar about his neck, the guard took posts about the chariot of the Queen, and Tarzan was led a few yards in advance of it. Then the keepers brought Belthar closer to him, holding him just out of reach but only with difficulty, for when the irascible beast recognized the ape-man he flew into a frenzy of rage that taxed the eight men to hold him at all.

Warriors were deploying on either side of a wide lane leading toward the north from the chariot of Nemone. In solid ranks they formed on either side of this avenue, facing toward its center, their spear points dropped to form a wall of steel against the lion should he desert the chase and break to right or left. Behind them, craning necks to see above the shoulders of the fighting men, the populace pushed and shoved for advantageous points from which to view the spectacle.

A noble approached Tarzan. He was Phordos, the father of Gemnon, hereditary captain of the hunt for the rulers of Cathne. He came quite close to Tarzan and spoke to him in a low whisper, "I am sorry that I must have a part in this," he said, "but my office requires it," and then aloud, "In the name of the Queen, silence! These are the rules of the grand hunt of Nemone, Queen of Cathne: The quarry shall move north down the center of the lane of warriors; when he has proceeded a hundred paces the keepers shall unleash the hunting lion, Belthar; let no man distract the lion from the chase or aid the quarry, under penalty of death. When the lion has killed and while he is feeding let the keepers, guarded by warriors, retake him."

Then he turned to Tarzan. "You will run straight north until Belthar overtakes you," he said.

"What if I elude him and escape?" demanded the ape-man. "Shall I have my freedom then?"

Phordos shook his head sadly. "You will not escape him," he said. Then he turned toward the Queen and knelt. "All is in readiness, your majesty. Shall the hunt commence?"

Nemone looked quickly about her. She saw that the guards were so disposed that she might be protected in the event that the lion turned back; she saw that slaves from her stables carried great nets with which Belthar was to be retaken after the hunt. She knew and they knew that not all of them would return alive to Cathne, but that would but add to the interest and excitement of the day. She nodded her head to Phordos. "Let the lion scent the quarry once more; then the hunt may start," she directed.

The keepers let Belthar move a little closer to the ape-man, but not before they had enlisted the aid of a dozen additional men to prevent his dragging the original eight until he was within reach of the quarry.

Nemone leaned forward eagerly, her eyes upon the savage beast that was the pride of her stable; the light of insanity gleamed in them now. "It is enough!" she cried. "Belthar knows him now, nor will he ever leave his trail until he has tracked him down and killed him, until he has reaped his reward and filled his belly with the flesh of his kill, for there is no better hunting lion in all Cathne than Belthar."

Along the gantlet of warriors that the quarry and the lion were to run spears had been stuck into the ground at intervals, and floating from the hafts of these were different colored pennons. The populace, the nobles, and the Queen had laid wagers upon the color of the pennon nearest which they thought the kill would occur, and they were still betting when Phordos slipped the collar from Tarzan's neck.

In a hollow near the river that runs past Cathne a lion lay asleep in dense brush, a mighty beast with a yellow coat and a great black mane. Strange sounds coming to him from the plain disturbed him, and he rumbled complainingly in his throat; but as yet he seemed only half awake. His eyes were closed, but his half wakefulness was only seeming. Numa was awake, but he wanted to sleep and was angry with the men-things that were disturbing him. They were not too close as yet; but he knew that if they came closer he would have to get up and investigate, and that he did not want to do; he felt very lazy.

Out on the field Tarzan was striding along the spear-bound lane. He counted his steps, knowing that at the hundredth Belthar would be loosed upon him. The ape-man had a plan. Across the river to the east was the forest in which he had hunted with Xerstle and Pindes and Gemnon; could he reach it, he would be safe. No lion or no man could hope ever to overtake the lord of the jungle once he swung to the branches of those trees.

But could he reach the wood before Belthar overtook him? Tarzan was swift, but there are few creatures as swift as Numa at the height of his charge. With a start of a hundred paces, the ape-man felt that he might outdistance an ordinary lion; but Belthar was no ordinary lion. He was the result of generations of breeding that had resulted in the power of sustaining great speed for a much longer time than would have been possible for a wild lion, and of all the hunting lions of Cathne Belthar was the best.

At the hundredth pace Tarzan leaped forward at top speed. Behind him he heard the frenzied roar of the hunting lion as his leashes were slipped and, mingling with it, the roar of the crowd.

Smoothly and low ran Belthar, the hunting lion, swiftly closing up the distance that separated him from the quarry. He looked neither to right nor to left; his fierce, blazing eyes remained fixed upon the fleeing man ahead.

Behind him rolled the chariot of the Queen, the drivers goading their lions to greater speed that Nemone might be in at the kill, yet Belthar outdistanced them as though they were rooted to the ground. The Queen, in her excitement, was standing erect, screaming encouragement to Belthar. Her eyes blazed scarcely less fiercely than those of the savage carnivore she cheered on; her bosoms rose and fell to her excited breathing; her heart raced with the racing death ahead. The Queen of Cathne was consumed by the passion of love turned to hate.

The nobles, the warriors, and the crowd were streaming after the chariot of the Queen. Belthar was gaining on the quarry when Tarzan turned suddenly to the east toward the river after he had passed the end of the gantlet that had held him to a straight path at the beginning of his flight.

A scream of rage burst from the lips of Nemone as she saw and realized the purpose of the quarry. A sullen roar rose from the pursuing crowd. They had not thought that the hunted man had a chance, but now they understood that he might yet reach the river and the forest. This, of course, did not mean to them that he would then escape, for they well knew that Belthar would pursue him across the river; what they feared was that they might be robbed of the thrills of witnessing the kill.

But presently their anger turned to relief as they saw that Belthar was gaining on the man so rapidly that there was no chance that the latter might reach the river before he was overhauled and dragged down.

Tarzan, too, glancing back over a bronzed shoulder, realized that the end was near. The river was still two hundred yards away and the lion, steadily gaining on him, but fifty.

Then the ape-man turned and waited. He stood at ease, his arms hanging at his side; but he was alert and ready. He knew precisely what Belthar would do, and he knew what he would do. No amount of training would have changed the lion's instinctive method of attack; he would rush at Tarzan, rear upon his hind feet when close, seize him with his taloned paws and drive his great fangs through his head or neck or shoulder; then he would drag him down and devour him.

But Tarzan had met the charge of lions before. It would not be quite so easy for Belthar as Belthar and the screaming audience believed, yet the ape-man guessed that, without a knife, he could do no more than delay the inevitable. He would die fighting, however; and now, as Belthar charged growling upon him, he crouched slightly and answered the roaring challenge of the carnivore with a roar as savage as the lion's.

Suddenly he detected a new note in the voice of the crowd, a note of surprise and consternation. Belthar was almost upon him as a tawny body streaked past the ape-man, brushing his leg as it came from behind him; and as Belthar rose upon his hind feet fell upon him, a fury of talons and gleaming fangs, a great lion with a golden coat and a black mane—a mighty engine of rage and destruction.

Roaring and growling, the two great beasts rolled upon the ground as they tore at one another with teeth and claws while the astounded ape-man looked on and the chariot of the Queen approached, and the breathless crowd pressed forward.

The strange lion was larger than Belthar and more powerful, a giant of a lion in the full prime of his strength and ferocity; and he fought as one inspired by all the demons of Hell. Presently Belthar gave him an opening; and his great jaws closed upon the throat of the hunting lion of Nemone, jaws that drove mighty fangs through the thick mane of his adversary, through hide and flesh deep into the jugular of Belthar; then he braced his feet and shook Belthar as a cat might shake a mouse, breaking his neck.

Dropping the carcass to the ground, the victor faced the astonished Cathneans with snarling face; then he slowly backed to where the ape-man stood and stopped beside him, and Tarzan laid his hand upon the black mane of Jad-bal-ja, the Golden Lion.

For a long moment there was unbroken silence as the two faced the enemies of the lord of the jungle, and the awed Cathneans only stood and stared; then a woman's voice rose in a weird scream. It was Nemone. Slowly she stepped from her golden car and amidst utter silence walked toward the carcass of the dead Belthar while her people watched her, motionless and wondering.

She stopped with her sandalled feet touching the bloody mane of the hunting lion and gazed down upon the dead carnivore. She might have been in silent prayer for the minute that she stood there; then she raised her head suddenly and looked about her. There was a wild gleam in her eyes and she was very white, white as the ivory ornament in the hollow of her throat.

"Belthar is dead!" she screamed, and whipping her dagger from its sheath drove its glittering point deep into her own heart. Without a sound she sank to her knees and toppled forward across the body of the dead Belthar.

*   *   *

As the moon rose, Tarzan placed a final rock upon a mound of earth beside the river that runs to Cathne through the valley of Onthar.

The warriors and the nobles and the people had followed Phordos to the city to empty the dungeons of Nemone and proclaim Alextar King, leaving their dead Queen lying at the edge of the Field of the Lions with the dead Belthar.

The human service they had neglected the beast-man had performed, and now beneath the soft radiance of an African moon he stood with bowed head beside the grave of a woman who had found happiness at last.

ABOUT EDGAR RICE BURROUGHS

Edgar Rice Burroughs is one of the world's most popular authors. With no previous experience as an author, he wrote and sold his first novel—*A Princess of Mars*—in 1912. In the ensuing thirty-eight years until his death in 1950, Burroughs wrote 91 books and a host of short stories and articles. Although best known as the creator of the classic *Tarzan of the Apes* and *John Carter of Mars*, his restless imagination knew few bounds. Burroughs' prolific pen ranged from the American West to primitive Africa and on to romantic adventure on the moon, the planets, and even beyond the farthest star.

No one knows how many copies of ERB books have been published throughout the world. It is conservative to say, however, that of the translations into 32 known languages, including Braille, the number must run into the hundreds of millions. When one considers the additional world-wide following of the Tarzan newspaper feature, radio programs, comic magazines, motion pictures and television, Burroughs must have been known and loved by literally a thousand million or more.

Read
Edgar Rice
Burroughs'
classic novels of the
titled English Lord,
who was raised by apes
in the jungles of Africa.